JUSTICE DIVIDED

THE COWBOY JUSTICE ASSOCIATION
BOOK TEN

By Olivia Jaymes

www.OliviaJaymes.com

Justice Divided

It's just another normal day with the twins when Ava gets a frantic call from her sister. Mary's husband Lyle Bryson has been shot dead and she's the main suspect. She needs Ava to come home to Corville right away.

Pressed back into service to find the killer of his half-brother, Logan finds himself once again at odds with the family. With Ava's sister under a cloud of suspicion, it feels like the last time he put a Bryson behind bars.

But neither Logan nor Ava believes that Mary killed Lyle. Jumping at the chance to work with her husband again, Ava is determined to clear her sister's name. But as more secrets are revealed, having a killer in the family might be the least of their problems…

CHAPTER ONE

"And they all lived happily ever after."

Ava Wright whispered the last sentence of the story and quietly closed the book. She leaned down to press a light kiss on her daughter's forehead and push a curl back from her silky cheek. The innocence of childhood.

Brianna loved the stories about princesses and heroes that saved the damsels in distress. She thought every book ended with everyone falling in love and having a party. Ava could only hope it would be a long time before her daughter realized that wasn't the case. Let her enjoy her youth as long as possible. A six-year-old should believe in fairies and magic and unicorns and rainbows.

Ava wished she still did, too. But a person couldn't stay innocent and naive and write murder mysteries. Having a husband that dealt with deadly crime didn't help the situation either. She'd had to institute a rule against putting crime scene photos where little hands and big eyes could find them. They were now banished to a file cabinet in the office under lock and key.

She tiptoed out of her daughter's bedroom, hoping that this

story would stick for the night. While her twin brother Colt was a good sleeper, Brianna was a night owl and it usually took two or three extra books to get her to finally fall asleep. She took after Ava in that way. There were too many exciting things going on to waste time sleeping.

Placing the book on the bookshelf in the living room, Ava padded on bare feet into the kitchen. It had been a long day and a glass of wine sounded like the perfect antidote to her own sleepless nights. She never slept well when her husband Logan wasn't next to her. Lately that was more often than not. It wasn't what she'd envisioned when they were married but he loved his job, just as much as she loved hers. They'd agreed the travel was a reasonable tradeoff to get him out of the line of fire as a sheriff. She had to repeatedly remind herself that this job was safer. Busy but safe.

Some days she missed Logan being the sheriff of Corville. At least he'd had regular hours and deputies to help him out. Of course, people had shot at him back then and that wasn't so great.

But he was supposed to come home tonight, although his flight had been delayed due to fog in Denver. She'd placed his dinner in the refrigerator but it would reheat nicely in the microwave.

Pouring a glass of Chardonnay, she settled on the couch, balancing her laptop on her thighs. She'd been doing edits this week, so she might as well get some work done while she waited for her husband to get home.

She didn't know how long she'd been heads down at work but the sound of a key in the door brought her back to the present. Rubbing her stiff neck, she heard two voices, Logan and an unfamiliar feminine one, drifting in from the foyer. Setting her computer aside, Ava rose quickly to see who was with her husband. He hadn't mentioned bringing anyone home.

"Hey, honey. I need to get Kim a file from the office. Ava, this is our newest employee Kim. Kim, this is my wife Ava."

Logan hurried by, dropping a kiss on Ava's lips before he disappeared down the hall to the spare bedroom-slash-office.

So *this* was Kim. Ava had been hearing quite a bit about the woman for the last few months. In fact, it seemed like every other sentence out of Logan's mouth started with the name Kim. She was completely and utterly tired of hearing about this female who from what she'd heard – in exhaustive detail – had an excellent record in law enforcement with several murder cases under her belt.

She was younger than Ava had expected. Taller, too. Pretty, if you liked the buxom blonde-haired blue-eyed type. Logan sure had before he'd married her, despite the fact that Ava was not blonde and not tall. Her rack wasn't bad, though, although childbirth and breastfeeding had taken their toll. Suddenly Ava wished she was dressed in something a little more fancy than a pair of khaki shorts and a t-shirt. Despite spending hours on a plane and in airports, Kim looked cool and put together in a pair of slim black slacks and a crisp white blouse.

"It's nice to meet you," Ava said, remembering her manners. "I've heard so many good things about your work. Can I get you something to drink? We can sit down in the living room if you like. You must be exhausted."

The younger woman smiled and shook her head. "Thank you but I'm afraid I just need that file and then to be on my way. It is nice to meet you finally. Logan talks about you and the twins all the time. You're just like he described."

Really? You're nothing like he described.

"I'd introduce you to the kids but they're asleep." They'd run out of conversation quickly, but then the only thing they had in common was Logan. And maybe a fascination with murder. "What file is Logan getting for you?"

"The Chatsman murder," Logan answered from behind her, bumping her slightly – and on purpose – as he walked by. He gave her a playful wink before turning back to his employee in training. "Here you go. The photos are in there so take a look and let me know if you see anything."

Kim accepted the folder and slipped it inside her briefcase. "Thanks. I'll go through the file tonight."

Logan shook his head. "If you want to sleep, you won't. Those photos redefine grisly. Might want to wait until the light of day."

Kim shrugged and moved toward the front door. "Nothing bothers me. I have a strong stomach and a great home security system. But thanks for the warning. I'll call you in the morning."

Oh goody. Ava was worried Logan might go more than twelve hours without speaking to his protégé.

Protector that her husband was, he watched as Kim climbed into her car and drove away. Then he turned around and slammed the door shut behind him, flipping the lock before bearing down on Ava and lifting her into a gigantic hug.

"Woman, you cannot know how much I missed you. Did you miss me?"

They had a running joke about this.

Giving him a coy smile, she looked up at him from under her lashes. "Well…I was pretty busy."

Logan threw back his head and laughed, although not as loud as he would have if the twins had been awake. Pulling her closer, he leaned down to nuzzle her neck, running his nose along her jawline. Even after all these years and two kids, Ava was helpless when her husband got amorous. A shiver ran through her and she closed her eyes as his lips found that spot on her neck that made her insane. He knew it too, the sexy bastard.

"I wouldn't expect anything different, my good girl. I don't know what I want more, you or dinner. I'm starved for you both."

Trying to hold onto a shred of sanity, Ava struggled for breath. "What is Kim looking for in the Chatsman file?"

She and Logan had been through every open case with a fine-toothed comb. The Chatsman case had few leads and less evidence. A respected businessman had been murdered while he worked late at the office. Gutted like a fish. Logan hadn't been kidding about the crime scene photos. Ugly stuff.

Unfortunately, everyone that had a motive had a rock solid alibi, and everyone that didn't have a good alibi didn't have a motive. It was a recipe for frustration.

"She thinks she might have seen a similar murder in Seattle," he said, his lips against her skin. "She's going to look over the file and photos."

Ava pulled back from her husband. "You think it's a serial?"

Chuckling, Logan pressed a soft kiss against her lips. "Thank God I have decent self-esteem, because if I didn't you would have shredded it by now. You're more excited about a serial murder case than your husband, even when he's been gone for a week."

"That's not true," Ava protested, feeling the warmth invade her cheeks. "It's just kind of cool, that's all."

"Is it cool that I'm home?"

Easy question. "Way cool. How about we warm up your dinner and you can tell me all about the case you closed."

Logan waggled his eyebrows and reached down to give her bottom a squeeze. He was still her horndog. When it came to him, she was one, too. "And then we can go to bed?"

"All night long," Ava promised, enjoying the hot look in her husband's eyes. He was raring to go. Neither of them would get much sleep tonight, but then they rarely did when he first returned from a business trip. "Go kiss the kids on their foreheads while I toss your dinner in the microwave. But if you wake 'em up, you're dealing with them until they go back to sleep."

"I'll be as quiet as a mouse," he promised as he headed back down the hall, this time to see his children. The twins would be thrilled to see their dad in the morning. On his first day back, he always made them chocolate chip pancakes. Ava had a feeling it was something that Logan's mother had made him when he was small.

It was kind of funny, but the house always seemed warmer and brighter when Logan was home. All snug, her entire family was together. It was something that was happening less and less these days. She'd enjoy it while she had it.

CHAPTER TWO

A va groaned as she placed sliced apples in each of the twins'
lunchboxes. Logan was having another go at his favorite
subject. "We don't need a dog. In fact, the very last thing we
need is a dog. I've been through potty training and I don't have a
deep-seated need to housebreak a puppy."

"I'd help," Logan protested indignantly. "It wouldn't be that
bad. All kids need a dog and it would teach them responsibility."

The old "the kids would help take care of the pet" ploy. Her
own mother had fallen for this when Ava had been around ten.
Of course, it had been Ava's mother who had ended up taking
care of their dog Lazarus. Lazarus had certainly been loyal to
Carol Hayworth as well. He'd followed at her heels every day
that he'd been on this earth. Ava's mother had been heartbroken
when Lazarus passed on.

The last thing I need is something else to feed and take care of.

Reining in her impatience, Ava snapped the lids on the
lunchboxes closed. The carpool would be here any minute and
the kids were still brushing their teeth. One tooth at a time.
Slowly. While Ava applauded their efforts at dental hygiene, their
pace could sometimes make her crazy when she was trying to get

them to summer day camp on time. Or anywhere, for that matter.

"You and I both know that Brianna and Colt aren't ready for the responsibility of a pet. They can barely dress themselves. They're six years old. I'd be the one that would end up taking care of a puppy."

"I said I would help."

Finally the twins scampered into the kitchen just as the carpool pulled up into the driveway. Ava slipped their lunches into their backpacks and both she and Logan gave kisses and hugs before they trotted away and off to day camp with their friends. They'd have a morning of arts and crafts, soccer, and video games – if it rained. They absolutely loved going and as a bonus it gave her four hours of quiet.

She returned to the kitchen and sighed at the mess. Logan had indeed made pancakes this morning and it looked like a tornado had hit their kitchen. It didn't improve her rapidly declining mood. He needed to drop the puppy thing.

"A dog is a lot of work."

Refilling his coffee cup, Logan gave her his patented wicked grin. "We could just have another baby instead."

He wasn't getting it and she had to resist the urge to reach out and smack his forehead. Hard.

"We need another child like we need holes drilled in our heads. You're never home," she replied sharply, grabbing the batter bowl and beginning to rinse it. "And yes, I know you're trying to be home more but that hasn't happened. I'm barely able to find time to work now even with the kids finally starting school or going to morning camp. Can you imagine the chaos around here if we had another baby and a dog?"

They'd have to sedate me.

Ava loved her husband and children more than her own life.

There wasn't anything she wouldn't do for them, but she was an introvert at heart. She needed a few minutes of peace each day to recharge her batteries. Just five or ten. Logan was talking about taking the small amount of time she had each day to get shit done and tossing it out the window.

"I'm really trying to be home more." Logan took the bowl out of her hands and placed it by the sink before turning her to face him. "I meant it when I said that I would be and I'm going to make it happen. I know you have it rough when I'm gone all the time and that it isn't fair. Believe me, I worry about that. I'm just asking for a little more time. Now go take a shower and let me handle these dishes. When I'm home, everything isn't your responsibility."

For a moment Ava was going to argue and then realized he was right. It was force of habit to do it all herself, taking the world onto her shoulders, but Logan was standing next to her and he'd made the mess. He could clean it up.

She wasn't even going to tell him how to clean it up, although she was sorely tempted. She'd learned soon after the twins were born that supervising him changing a diaper wasn't a great way to get him to do it. He did things in his own way. Just because she wouldn't use that spray cleaner to wipe up the countertops didn't mean it was wrong.

Although it totally was. But I've learned to keep quiet.

She allowed him to push her toward the bedroom where she stripped off her yoga pants and t-shirt before stepping under the hot, steamy spray of the shower. A sigh escaped her lips and her muscles loosened as the water beat against her lower back. Resting her head against the wet tile she allowed herself to relax for the first time today.

She really ought to apologize to her husband. She'd been snippy with him and she didn't mean to. Sometimes the stress of things got to her. She was trying so hard to be everything to everyone and Logan kept telling her she was taking on too much. She didn't need to be a room mother and volunteer for the PTA. She didn't need to take on such an ambitious writing schedule. Add in Brianna's dance class and Colt's soccer club and she was getting hardly anything done all that well. It was all suffering and she needed to reevaluate what was really important.

The slam of the bathroom door made her jump and she whirled around just as the sexiest man she'd ever seen opened the shower door while he efficiently stripped out of his clothes. Her mouth watered at the sight of those flat abs and what lay just below. He'd kept her up half the night last night celebrating his homecoming, but it looked like he wasn't done.

Lucky me. A couple of orgasms are just what I need.

Logan quirked that sexy eyebrow and his gaze swept her from head to toe. "How about a little company?"

Since he wasn't wearing any clothes, Ava reached out for the only handle that was handy, her hand wrapping around the base of his cock.

"You can come in if you wash my back."

They were going to empty the hot water heater this morning.

Logan had been gone too damn long. He hated being away from his family and with every trip his impatience with traveling grew. This trip had only been a week long, but it might as well have been a month. He'd missed so many things with his family, but he'd also missed...this.

Pressing Ava against the tiles of the shower, he could feel her body flush against his. Her pert breasts with their rock hard nipples, the curve of her belly, and her sexy legs which were beginning to part ever so slightly in anticipation of what he might have in store for her. She might have believed he'd assuaged his pent-up hunger last night but it wasn't even close. He'd never get enough of this woman.

The hot steam billowed around them as he kissed his way down her body, starting at the hollow of her neck and ending around her bellybutton, making her squirm with delight. Her fingers carded through his now wet hair and she held on as he insinuated himself between her thighs, lifting one onto his shoulder. His questing fingers found her wet and ready but he wanted her screaming for it. There was nothing in the world so wonderful as Ava saying his name as she orgasmed.

She braced her hands on his shoulders as his tongue went to work. She cried out as he flicked over her clit a few times, but he wasn't inclined to make this short and sweet. Lazily, he drew his tongue along her folds until she was panting, her nails digging into his flesh.

Glancing up he could see her head lolled to the side, her eyes closed and her lips parted as she struggled for breath. Water cascaded down her body, creating the most beautiful human waterfall effect he'd ever seen. He might have watched it in fascination all morning but his own cock was hard, throbbing, and making demands. After last night he ought to have more control, but he was as horny and ready as a teenager. The blood pounded in his ears like a freight train and the pressure in his lower back built to a crescendo.

Short and sweet isn't so bad.

"I love you, Ava."

This time he went in for the kill, his tongue doing devilish things to her swollen clit until she shattered into a million pieces, crying out his name as she fell apart. Her legs gave out and he caught her, keeping her from falling into a heap at the bottom of the shower. Standing, he lifted her off of the floor and wrapped her legs around his waist as he pressed his cock into her waiting warmth. Tight. Like silk.

Somewhere in the back of his mind, he knew he'd been with women before Ava but damned if he could remember even one of them. She'd made it so they didn't even exist. She'd taken over every facet of his life and heart and he wouldn't have it any other way.

They clung to each other as he pistoned in and out of her, the only sounds the splashing of water and their ragged breaths and moans. Ava urged him on. Faster. Harder. A frisson of electricity ran down his spine and he knew he had only moments left. Reaching between them he placed his thumb on her already sensitive button and rubbed soft circles around it.

Her explosion came on the heels of his own and he had to concentrate to keep from falling to his knees. They didn't move for a long time, content to simply be as close as they could possibly be. Eventually their heartbeats slowed and their breathing evened out. Logan lowered Ava's feet to the tile floor, holding her until he was sure she could stand on her own.

"Baby, we should do this more often."

Laughing, Ava leaned against the tile wall, her hands still stroking his chest and arms. If he were a cat he'd purr with contentment.

"If you were home more, we would."

Consider it done, good girl.

CHAPTER THREE

T he aggravating sound of Logan's ringtone pierced the air, ending their morning of sex and quiet. Ava knew that sound all too well. It was work. So much for having a few days off. With her luck lately, he'd be back on the road before dinnertime.

Rolling over on the bed, he grimaced and then grabbed his cell from the side table.

"Sorry, baby."

The problem was he really was truly sorry. He didn't want to leave any more than she wanted him to but when duty called he had to answer it. They'd made a deal, after all. No more guns pointed at him. It was hard to be pissed off when he didn't appear any happier about this phone call than she did. She pondered rolling over and taking a nap before the kids returned home but her own cell phone was ringing on the other nightstand. Levering up and wrapping a robe around her rapidly cooling body, she checked the screen display.

Her mother.

At least it wasn't a Skype call. One look at Ava's flushed cheeks and tumbled hair and Carole Hayworth would know exactly what her youngest daughter had been doing.

To give Logan his privacy for a business call, Ava quickly exited the bedroom and headed for the kitchen. A glass of iced tea sounded like the perfect after-sex cocktail on a Tuesday morning.

"Hey, Mom. What's going on?"

"Thank heavens you answered." Carol sounded agitated and out of breath, as if she'd been running up and down the stairs, which would be unusual behavior for the doting mother and grandmother. "You need to come here right away."

Ava hadn't been back to Corville since she and Logan had moved to the outskirts of Seattle. They were closer to his partner Jared and the Seattle office. At least that's what they'd told themselves when they'd made the move. Her parents normally visited them, not the other way around.

"Okay, Mom. Calm down. What's happening? Why do I need to come home?"

There was a pause and then an audible deep breath. "I'm sorry, I'm just so upset. Lyle is dead, Ava. They found his body this morning."

Lyle Bryson. Ava's brother-in-law.

"Wait…he's…dead?"

The last time she'd seen Lyle, which admittedly had been quite a while ago, he'd been in perfect health. He ran five miles a day.

They found his body this morning.

That sounded ominous, but it was probably just her murder mystery mind.

"Yes, he's gone," Carol announced loudly, her voice rising higher with emotion. "And the police are here asking questions. Your sister is beside herself with grief. She needs her family here. We need you."

One word jumped out to Ava's sluggish brain. *Police.*

"The police are there? What are they asking about?"

It was probably just routine and her sister Mary was being overly dramatic as she often was. No one could play the victim more than Ava's sister, although this time she had a good reason.

"Lyle's death, of course."

This conversation was beginning to go around in circles.

"Mom, just where did they find Lyle's body?"

"On the jogging trail in the park. Another runner found him."

Geez, maybe running really did kill him.

"Then I'm sure the cops are just asking the usual questions. Nothing to be concerned with. But as soon as Logan gets off the phone I'll talk to him about coming home for the funeral. Of course, we'll be there to support Mary."

Another noisy exhale from her mother. "I'm rattled and I'm not making myself clear here. They're asking Mary questions about Lyle because of the way he died. He was shot."

Shot? Lyle was shot? This was beginning to look like déjà vu all over again. Bill Bryson – Lyle's father – had been shot a little more than eight years ago at a wedding reception.

Despite that being the case that brought Ava and Logan together, it had also been a cluster in a myriad of other ways, ruining many lives. Lyle's was one of them. In the end, Ava and Logan had decided to move out of Corville.

"Ava?"

Logan's voice penetrated her thoughts of the past and she looked up to see him standing in the kitchen doorway wearing an extremely unhappy expression. He didn't know the half of it yet. The last thing he wanted to do was go back to his hometown.

Logan held up his phone. "It's Jason. Drake in Corville is

asking for our help in a murder investigation."

I know exactly what murder they're talking about. Do you?

"Mom, I'm going to have to call you back."

✧   ✧   ✧   ✧

What a fucking mess.

Logan had Jason in one ear begging him to go back to Corville to help his former deputy – now sheriff – Drake with a murder investigation and Ava in the other telling him that her mother had called panicked and upset. Both of them were explaining just who the victim was.

Lyle.

Ava's brother-in-law. Or Logan's half-brother, depending on how one looked at it. The day Logan had found out that the late Bill Bryson was his real father the news hadn't been welcomed. It had changed everything and had led to finding out hard truths that the town of Corville had never wanted to know. When Logan had resigned as sheriff and moved his family away there had been a collective sigh of relief. He was a constant reminder of the tiny hamlet's sins. He'd uncovered the bodies – literally – and they couldn't forgive that.

"I'm going to need to discuss this with Ava." Logan wanted to put an end to the call with Jason. "This isn't just my decision. I'll call you back."

He didn't let Jason try to persuade him further, quickly disconnecting the call before his friend could say anything else. At this point, there wasn't much to say. Logan already knew what he had to do but it didn't mean that he had to go quietly with a goddamn smile on his face.

"That was Jason."

Ava nodded, opening the fridge and retrieving two bottles of water, one of which she handed to him. "You said that."

"He wants me to go to Corville to help Drake out with Lyle's murder."

"You said that, too."

His wife normally didn't hide how she was feeling about things, at least not with him. But right now, she could have been holding a pair of deuces or a royal flush.

"We have to go," he heard himself saying out loud. "I mean...it's family. We have to go if only for the funeral."

He wasn't looking forward to it, though. Lots of people looking at him, staring and whispering when he walked by. When he'd left, he hadn't thought about what it would be like to return. Somehow he'd fooled himself into thinking he'd never have to.

I'm a fucking idiot.

"Agreed. As much as Mary and I have issues, I can't let her go through this alone."

"I bet your sister is being insufferable now."

Shit, he shouldn't have said that. Jesus, she was a widow. He should be saying nice things about her and Lyle. He should want to be loving and supportive, but it was difficult when Mary hated his guts. She was damn vocal about it, too. She still blamed him for the Bryson family losing their business and a large chunk of the family fortune. Never mind that it was the oldest brother Wade who had turned into a serial killer. Somehow Logan was worse.

"I think...I think she really loved him. For all of Mary's faults, she was sweet to Lyle."

Leave it to his wonderful wife to find the good in a person. Mary had been a royal bitch to Ava as well, but somehow she always seemed to rise above her sister's behavior and simply smile in response.

Logan sighed and fell down into a kitchen chair, his head

lolling back. He was supposed to be getting a few well-deserved days off and now he had to deal with this shit.

"I feel sorry for her, I truly do. It's just not easy because I wouldn't say she and I have ever been close."

Or even nice to one another. Mary had done her damnedest to talk Ava out of marrying Logan and that was something he couldn't forget.

Then there was the whole issue he hadn't even begun to deal with, still numb after hearing the news. His half-brother had been shot in cold blood. The Bryson family had many faults, but Lyle hadn't been one of them. A truly good guy, Lyle had worked hard and given back to the community. He sure as hell hadn't deserved to come to a bloody end like that.

It didn't matter whether Mary liked Logan or not. Helping Drake find Lyle's killer wouldn't necessarily be for her. It would be for Lyle.

"I'm going to tell Jason I'll do it."

"I know."

His wife was currently making another pot of coffee. What he really needed was a shot of whiskey, but it was a little early in the day.

"You think you know everything about me."

Chuckling, she pressed the start button and turned to him, her hands massaging his tense shoulders. He rested his head on her belly and sighed when her fingers found a particularly tight spot at the base of his neck.

"I don't think I know everything, but I have observed a few things in our years of marriage. One, you would never turn down a friend that asked you for help. Drake is a friend. Two, you liked Lyle, although he was angry with you after you put Wade behind bars. Let's just say it was an educated guess and leave it at that."

Her fingers smoothed over his cheeks, her thumbs gently sweeping over his closed eyes. Everything was as shitty as could be but when he was like this with Ava it was all okay. She made his whole life better. So many people had been shocked when he'd married her, but he couldn't imagine his life without her. He'd do anything for her.

Even accept a new position at the consulting firm. It was more management and much less hands on, but it meant that he would be home almost all the time. Very little travel. It wasn't his dream job, but it meant that he could be home with his family more. He could help Ava and be there when times were tough. He could watch his children grow up for a change. Hell, they might even get a dog.

All he had to do was finish training his replacement Kim. She was doing a good job, but they were all afraid she was going to miss working in a big city police station. Hopefully it would all work out, but he hadn't mentioned it to Ava yet. He didn't want to get her hopes up when it was all still up in the air.

With any luck this would be his last field case. One more. Go to Corville, find a killer, and then give Ava the good news that he was going to be home every night for supper.

If only he didn't have to go back there. It was literally the last thing he wanted to do.

CHAPTER FOUR

T he twins scrambled ahead of them into the house, anxious to see inside of a home they didn't remember but had heard their parents talk about. Ava and Logan had held onto their home in Corville for various reasons – the real estate market, wanting a place to stay if they visited Ava's family, the ability to rent it out. But none of them were the whole truth. Ava suspected that Logan wanted a home near his mother's grave, but he wouldn't admit it. Eventually Ava's parents had split up and Carol Hayworth had moved in to the house temporarily until she had found her own place. She still had a key though and checked on the home regularly.

Carol was standing in the doorway with her arms outspread, ready to hug her grandchildren and give them kisses. "Welcome back. Did you have a good drive?"

"I think we sang every Sesame Street song that exists," Ava laughed, getting a hug from her mother as well. "I know them all by heart."

"Maybe you can teach me too," Carol said to Colt and Brianna who were currently checking out the large great room that led into the kitchen. "I think I remember a few from when your mother was your age."

Both children stopped and frowned as if they couldn't believe that their mom had ever been young.

Ava rolled her eyes. "Yes, I was once your age. But I was a perfect little angel and never gave Mom a moment of trouble."

Carol snorted and headed into the kitchen. "You might want to see a doctor. Your memory seems to be more than a little faulty. Now…who wants cookies? I made chocolate chip."

"If they don't, I do," Logan declared, hefting the last of their bags into the house. "In fact, I don't think Colt and Brianna like chocolate chip. I think they hate it."

Logan knew perfectly well that the kids loved chocolate chip but he'd decided to have some fun with them.

"I do, too," Colt said, indignation in his tone. "Chocolate's my favorite."

Brianna pushed at her brother's shoulder. "Peanut butter is your favorite. Chocolate is my favorite."

"Is not."

"Is too."

They could do this all day.

"There's enough for everyone," Carol stated with a huge smile. "And juice, too. But first let's get you washed up."

The twins wanted to eat their cookies outside, so they set up the snack at the table on the back deck. Each one had two cookies and a cup of apple juice. Logan and Ava had opted for iced tea instead of juice, as had Carol.

"I want you to talk to Mary," Carol said when the children were finished with their cookies and had scampered off to play kickball in the backyard under the shade trees. It was a perfect summer day, warm and sunny but not too hot. "She's devastated that Lyle is gone but the police keep asking her questions. I'm hoping now that you're here for Logan to take charge of the investigation all of that will stop and she can grieve in peace."

"I will need to talk to her," Logan replied, his expression neutral. There hadn't been much love between Ava's husband and her sister. In fact, it was all they could do not to hiss at each other like angry cats. "She knows things about his friends, business partners, and his daily routines. Those are details we need to know to be able to effectively run this investigation."

"Of course," Carol agreed. "I just want the badgering to stop. When I was over there earlier today one of Drake's deputies kept asking her about her marriage to Lyle, suggesting that it was in trouble."

"Logan is going to have to ask that same question, Mom. It's standard procedure."

Carol didn't like the answer. "It's already been asked and answered. Multiple times. I don't understand why they keep doing it."

Because they don't believe Mary for some reason. Wonder why?

Luckily for Ava, she didn't have to respond to her mother. The sound of a male voice from the side of the house stopped their conversation and turned their attention to Drake James, the man who had taken over for Logan as Corville's sheriff.

"Hey Drake," Ava called with a wave of her hand. "It's good to see you. Sit down and have some cookies and iced tea."

Ava stood to fetch another glass, but Carol shook her head. "Let me get it. I need a refill, too."

Logan scooted his chair over to make room for Drake who was a big man, tall with wide shoulders. When he entered a room, he made an immediate impression. "Good timing. We arrived less than an hour ago."

Grimacing, Drake reached for a cookie from the platter. "About that…you were seen driving through town. That's how I knew you were here."

Logan muttered something under his breath that sounded suspiciously like "fucking small towns" but Ava stayed quiet. There was no use letting something that was inevitable bother them. They'd known this was going to happen and their presence was going to bring up a bunch of crap and gossip about the past. That's just how it was.

"I'm glad you're here, though," Drake said with a grin. "I've never been the lead on a murder and I don't want to let the citizens of Corville down. Lyle was well-liked in this community and everyone wants to see justice done."

Carol placed a glass of iced tea in front of Drake. "We certainly do. He was shot down in cold blood. Whoever did this needs to be behind bars for the rest of his life."

Logan drained the last of his glass. "I'm here to help. So tell me, what do we know so far?"

"Not a whole hell of a lot. No witnesses because it was so goddamn early in the morning. I had a couple of deputies scour the area for evidence but they didn't find anything. No one heard anything either. Another runner came up on his body and she called the cops. That's pretty much it. It's not much to go on."

"Have you pulled Lyle's finances?" Ava asked, her mystery writer hat firmly on. "Have you talked to Aaron?"

"Ava," Carol chided, sounding slightly outraged. "Are you suggesting that the cops comb through Mary and Lyle's private money affairs?"

Of course.

"It's stand—"

"Standard procedure," Carol finished for her. "I'm beginning to hate that phrase so I think I'll go inside. This conversation is upsetting."

"You definitely will hate it before this is over," Logan said.

"When a murder happens in the family all bets are off. Secrets are going to come out whether they like it or not. Nothing is sacred and I, better than most, should know that."

Leaning down, Carol dropped a kiss on Ava's forehead. "I think I'll find a good book and read. One with a happy ending."

Ava took a sip of her tea as her mother went into the house. "So you don't have any suspects?"

Drake rubbed his chin, his gaze not quite meeting hers. "I wouldn't say that we have *no* suspects."

Ava and Logan exchanged a glance. The hairs on her arm were standing straight at attention. The former deputy now sheriff couldn't look her in the eye. That wasn't like Drake James.

"You got someone in mind?" Logan finally asked, breaking the uncomfortable silence that had built up between them. "It's okay if it's just a hunch. I'm going to need to know."

Exhaling noisily, Drake winced and nodded. "Fine, it's Mary. There have been rumors around town about marital problems."

That was crazy talk. Mary? A murderer? She wouldn't want to mess up her manicure or her hair. Sure, she had a temper and could be mean but she wasn't a killer.

"And you think my sister decided to solve those problems by shooting her husband?"

"She owns a gun," Drake replied. "It matches the caliber of bullet the medical examiner pulled from the body."

That wasn't good. In fact, that was very bad. But he hadn't said it was a ballistics match. Just the same caliber. It would, however, probably be enough to get a warrant for Mary's gun.

"It's Montana, everyone owns a gun or several."

"We're getting ahead of ourselves here," Logan said, cutting off the debate. "We do this investigation by the book. We dot every I and cross every T. That means talking to your sister, but it also means casting a wide net for suspects. At this point, we don't know anything for sure."

"Then we better go talk to my sister."

Considering the state of the relationship between Ava and Mary, and Mary and Logan, this could get ugly really fast.

CHAPTER FIVE

C arol stayed with the twins while Logan and Ava went to see Mary. He wasn't looking forward to this. He and Mary had never liked each other and he didn't see an end to that anytime in the future. Like oil and water, they didn't mix and staying away from each other had been working perfectly.

"Try to be nice," Ava said as they knocked on Mary's front door. The house was lovely, a typical ranch style but a far cry from the luxury the Bryson family had enjoyed at one point. The practical minivan in the driveway didn't scream country club or ladies who lunch either. A large chunk of the Bryson fortune had gone to Wade's defense fund and what was left had been hollowed out by the lost business. Aaron and Lyle had been slowly building a new one.

"I'm always nice."

It was mostly true. Logan had met all kinds when he was sheriff and he'd learned not to take too much personally. Some people just loved to be unhappy and Mary Hayworth Bryson was one of them.

The door opened and Logan immediately tensed, seeing Ava's father Bruce on the other side of the threshold. Another of the Hayworth clan that wasn't thrilled when Ava had married Logan. He didn't bother to hide it either.

This should be interesting.

"About time you got here," Bruce growled at his daughter, ignoring Logan which was fine. The less Bruce and he interacted the better. "Your sister is distraught with grief."

Not bothering with pleasantries, Bruce turned on his heel and led the way into the cozy family room at the back of the house. A large overstuffed brown couch dominated the room along with a television that hung over the fireplace. Mary sat on the end of the sofa, sniffling into a sodden tissue, her eyes red-rimmed and swollen.

Ava immediately sat down next to her sister and placed an arm around the widow, whispering words of encouragement that Logan couldn't hear. Mary nodded as if she agreed but then burst into a fresh spate of tears, her shoulders shaking with her sobs.

Bruce's bushy brows were pulled together into a frown. "There's a pot of coffee in the kitchen. Lindsay made it."

Lindsay was Aaron's wife. Did that mean that Aaron was here as well? Logan wasn't quite ready to face his remaining half-brother that wasn't dead or in prison.

Deciding to ignore his father-in-law, Logan sat down on the other side of Mary. They needed to talk and putting it off for later wasn't going to help either of them.

"Mary, do you know why I'm here? Can you answer a few questions?"

She blew her nose and then nodded, dabbing at her wet cheeks. "Ava told me that you're going to help Sheriff Drake with the investigation."

"I'm going to do everything in my power to bring whoever did this to justice. You have my word on that."

Logan could have sworn he heard a snort from Bruce but he didn't bother to turn around, although his wife was giving her father a nasty look.

Ah...familial love and devotion.

"I need you to get the man that did this. He has to pay."

Interesting choice of words.

"What makes you think it's a man? Has there been someone giving Lyle a hard time? Did he have any enemies or piss off someone recently? Think about it, because even a small detail could be more important than you think."

Mary shook her head. "Everyone loved Lyle. He had lots of friends and no enemies."

"He was a good husband," Bruce's joined in. "The kind that takes care of his wife."

As opposed to me? A playboy with a bad reputation?

"Lyle was a good man." Logan wasn't going to argue the point because he agreed with it. His old friend had been a good person, which made this tragedy all the more a mystery. "He didn't deserve this, but I doubt this is a random act. I'm looking for the reason it happened. What about business? How was that going?"

"Better," Mary replied, a small smile crossing her face if only for a moment. "He was also doing real estate agent work and that was really picking up. He just sold a big house and earned a large commission."

"That's great. I want you to know that I'm going to be look-ing into the Bryson business and finances. It's standard procedure."

Just like that any friendly moment that Logan and Mary were having was gone. Scowling, her pale cheeks turned red with anger and her body stiffened, pushing Ava away.

"You're going to dig around in our lives? I don't think I can allow that. It's none of your business. I don't give a fuck about standard procedure."

"Mary, that's not how a lady speaks," her father admonished. Bruce was a stickler for propriety even when it didn't make any sense. Mary was grieving and angry and it was fine with Logan if she wanted to cuss him out.

"It's okay," Logan said. He was going to make her a hell of lot more angry by the time this conversation was done. "I'm also going to question you, your neighbors, your friends, and business associates so if there's something I need to know it's better that it comes directly from you. Is there anything you want to tell me?"

This was Mary's chance to tell him about their marital issues but from the mutinous expression on her face, she wasn't going to budge.

"I can't think of one thing I want to say to you."

Oh, I doubt that's true. I bet you have a bunch of stuff you'd like to say.

Logan lobbed the hand grenade and ducked for cover.

"Word around town is that you and Lyle were having troubles and thinking about splitting up."

The din of raised voices hurt Logan's ears. He was the father of twins, but they had nothing on Bruce and Mary when these two had their backs up. Ava was trying to calm them down, but Logan was content for them to continue to rant. If anything, they were talking and saying things they might not when they weren't so pissed off. So far Mary had admitted that she and Lyle had talked about divorce and that Lyle had even spent a few weeks sleeping at his brother's house. But they had decided to give their marriage another go.

Finally, he couldn't take the arguing anymore. Bruce kept telling Mary to be quiet and Ava kept trying to tell her father that he shouldn't interfere.

"Mary, I don't have any reason not to believe you." Logan raised his hands in mock surrender. "If you say that you and Lyle were reconciling then that's what happened."

Until someone or several someones tell me differently.

His declaration seemed to take the wind out of her sails, which was exactly what he'd hoped would happen.

"Well…good. It's the truth. I loved Lyle and he loved me."

"Of course, you did," Ava said in a soothing tone as if speaking to one of the twins when they were sick or upset. "Logan just has to ask these questions. It's hard, but the sooner we get this over with the better."

Bruce said something under his breath about it all being about Logan's career but luckily Ava didn't take the bait. Neither did Logan, of course. He'd learned early on how to navigate around his father-in-law.

Mary sniffed and patted her nose with the tissue. "I know that the town was talking about us, but every marriage goes through bad patches. That's all this was. Lyle and I were frustrated about…some things…and we had to work through it."

She was holding back, but at this point Logan wasn't going to force her to come clean. He'd only do that if he absolutely had to. Contrary to popular opinion in this room, he wasn't looking forward to interrogating her about their life, marriage, and the intimate details.

"Statistically the cops have to look at you," Logan reminded her. "They'd be derelict in their duty if they didn't. The best thing that can happen is to be investigated and then cleared. There won't be any cloud of suspicious that will follow you around. You don't want that."

Mary's fingers nervously shredded the sodden tissue. "You're going to head the investigation, right? Then you can help me."

Do you need help?

The words were on the tip of Logan's tongue, but he didn't utter them. It would only start a new argument.

"My goal is to find out who killed Lyle. I don't come into this case with any preconceived notions or suspicions. I'm open to any route that this takes me on."

Ava raised a brow at his politician-speak. "You have to do your part too, Mary. You need to cooperate with the police so they can clear you."

That went over like a turd in the punchbowl.

Bruce threw up his arms and began to pace the length of the living room. "Do they honestly think my little girl shot her husband? They have to be crazy. She wouldn't hurt a fly."

Nip this in the bud. Bruce wasn't a credible witness for Mary.

"Then we need to prove that," Logan stated firmly. "The police are trained not to take your word for it. They want evidence and that's what I'm here for. We need to find a way to exonerate Mary once and for all. For example, can anyone vouch for your whereabouts at the time of the murder?"

Mary shook her head. "I was in bed asleep. The sun was barely up."

Logan was about to follow up his question when he heard the clearing of a throat behind him.

Aaron and his wife Lindsay.

Lindsay hurried into the kitchen, but Aaron stood there silently before beckoning to Logan.

"We need to talk."

This day just kept getting better and better.

CHAPTER SIX

A va had never seen her sister so upset. Mary's mood swung wildly back and forth between anger at the police and life in general to sadness that Lyle was gone. In between there were bouts of disbelief that she was now a widow and alone.

"It's just so unfair," Mary wailed into a new tissue as fresh tears streamed down her cheeks. "My life wasn't supposed to turn out like this."

It certainly hadn't been Mary's plan, but life just laughed when mere human beings plotted out their futures.

Ava wasn't sure what to say to her sister. It wasn't fair and the whole situation was awful, but it didn't have to mean that her life was over.

"You'll make new plans," Ava said in her most calming voice. "You're young and have so much of life ahead of you. I'm sure that Lyle would want you to live a full life and enjoy yourself."

Mary's head jerked up, her brows pinched together. "How would you know what Lyle wanted? You've never come to visit us."

Would we have been welcome?

Ava doubted that Mary and Lyle would have rolled out the welcome mat for Logan. They still blamed him for their change in circumstances.

"Are you saying Lyle would want you to be miserable for the rest of your life?"

Appealing to logic probably wasn't the way to go here but what the heck.

"Of course not, but he'd want me to mourn. I'd want him to mourn if it was me that was shot."

"I'm not suggesting that you don't mourn. I'm simply saying that at some point in the future you may find yourself making new plans."

"Or I could be in prison," Mary replied, bitterness dripping from her tone. "The police have it out for me. Sheriff Drake kept asking questions about our marriage. He thinks I did it and I bet Logan does, too."

"Logan doesn't think that. He's looking for the actual killer and he won't be swayed by emotion. You're lucky he's on this case. He's had a great deal of experience with murder cases and his record is impeccable."

Mary's eyes narrowed. "I don't trust him. I need you to help me."

As flattered as Ava was to hear her sister finally ask for help, she wasn't thrilled with how Mary spoke about Logan.

"My husband is completely trustworthy. You can count on him to keep an open mind and find the person who did this awful thing."

But Mary was already shaking her head. "I only trust family."

"Logan is family," Ava pointed out. "He's your brother-in-law."

"Real family," Mary insisted. "Blood family. Will you do it? Will you look into this? Make sure the cops aren't taking shortcuts? You know about this stuff and I don't."

It wasn't as if Ava was planning to never discuss the case with Logan or not stick her nose into it anyway. If it gave Mary a little peace of mind...

"I'll keep my eyes open, but I can't promise anything."

"That's all I ask." Mary noisily blew her nose. "With you to keep an eye on the investigation, I know that it will be fair."

Ava doubted she had that kind of power when it came to the Corville sheriff's office, but Logan would see to it that the process was as fair and impartial as possible.

"It would be helpful if you could tell me more about Lyle's day to day life. His friends and business associates. That would give us a place to start."

Ava and Logan could work together again. It had been pretty fun the first time.

It had been years since Logan had seen or spoken to Aaron. He was well aware that the other man blamed him for the downfall of their family empire and also ripping off the mask of respectability the Bryson family wore. For the rest of his life Aaron would be known as the brother of a serial killer and that was Logan's fault.

Logan, however, wasn't one to shrink away from his accomplishments. He'd put the vigilante killer behind bars, and the fact that it was his half-brother Wade was simply a nasty part of the job. He was sad that Wade had turned out to be so evil and dark, but he needed to be put away for the safety of society. End of story. Aaron could be pissed off all he wanted but Logan couldn't change that.

"You wanted to talk to me?"

Aaron and Logan had stepped outside of the house, Logan

leaning against the front porch railing and Aaron sitting in a rocking chair. The tension between them was high and Logan wouldn't have been surprised if Aaron stood up and punched him in the face.

Aaron didn't beat around the bush, coming directly to the point. "Wade doesn't know yet."

Logan had assumed that a prison official would deliver the news, and then they'd put Wade into isolation for a few days so he didn't act out and hurt anyone. If he even cared. He hadn't exactly been communicative with the Bryson family since his arrest.

"Are you planning to tell him?"

Aaron had been staring at his shoes but he looked up at Logan to answer, their gazes clashing. "I was hoping you would go tell him."

That was...unexpected.

Logan stretched out his long legs, crossing one over the other, determined not to show how disturbed he was by the request. "Why me?"

"You're the only one that Wade respects. He refuses to see me or Lyle. He only allows his lawyers in there to work on his appeals. I haven't seen Wade since the sentencing."

This was the first Logan was hearing of this but then the Bryson family didn't keep him up to date on current events, especially when he'd made it clear he didn't want to be a Bryson.

"Considering Wade tried to kill me I'm not sure that I'd call his feelings for me respect. If I remember it correctly – and I do – he wanted me to die a slow and painful death."

"You're the only one he'll see."

Maybe.

"You don't know that he'll see me," Logan argued. "If he's not accepting visitors then he probably won't want to talk to me either. I'm the one that put him in prison, remember?"

Anger flashed in Aaron's eyes, but just for a moment. Apparently, he hadn't forgiven yet.

"I think about that every goddamn day."

Straightening, Logan wanted an end to this conversation as quickly as possible.

"I'm the bad guy. I'm the monster. Sure, your older brother was killing innocent people but somehow this is all my fault. I can see that."

Aaron sat back in the chair, steadily regarding Logan. Any friendship they may have shared long ago was gone. "Why did you have to be so good at your job? When you realized it was Wade, why didn't you let it go?"

Aaron didn't have a fucking clue.

"Because that's the Bryson way?" Logan jeered. "Family first and fuck everybody else. How's that working for you, buddy? Hell of a family motto to have. Embroider that shit on a pillow. I did my job and I put Wade where he belongs. If your business suffered or he spent too much money on his attorneys, then you need to talk to him about killing people. Shit, he shot your own damn father and uncle and here you sit, defending his ass."

"He's my brother."

"He's a cold-blooded killer," Logan shot back. "And trust me when I say that he doesn't give a shit about you. Or Lyle. Or anyone else. He's a goddamn sociopath who lacks empathy and the ability to form emotional bonds with others. If you look back on his life, you'll see that it's true. He acted as society expected him to but deep down he's only about Wade. He'd kill you if you were in his way and never have a guilty thought about it. You're wasting your time blaming me but go ahead if it makes you feel better."

The silence stretched on, the only sound the rustling of

leaves and the twittering of birds.

"I'm just here for Lyle. I'm going to find his killer and then I'll be gone. You won't have to see me again."

"This won't redeem you or anything."

Logan didn't think he needed any redemption. He slept fine at night.

"Didn't even cross my mind. So let's just get down to business. Do you know anyone that would have wanted to hurt Lyle? Anyone at all?"

Aaron shook his head. "No way. Everyone loved Lyle. He was a good guy and a good brother."

Even good people had secrets and enemies.

"What about husband? Was he a good one of those, too? Rumor has it that he and Mary had issues."

Rubbing his chin, a smile played around Aaron's lips. "They fought. They had problems. Just like everyone."

"Did Lyle talk about divorce?"

Aaron reluctantly nodded. "They did but I'm not sure he was serious about it."

"In any murder case, the spouse is under suspicion," Logan informed him. "So the first thing I want to do is investigate Mary and get her cleared."

"You don't think she did it?"

If Logan wasn't mistaken, Aaron sounded surprised. Interesting...

"I don't know...do you?"

Aaron shrugged like he didn't care one way or the other, which was bullshit.

"I think she's capable, but I don't think she did it."

Quite the admission. So much for circling the wagons around the family. Aaron had pretty much just thrown his sister-in-law under the bus.

"Many people are capable of murder but they don't actually do it."

Logan himself was capable but it wasn't something he aspired to. He bet Ava was capable too, if anyone threatened their children.

"I'm going to go where this investigation takes me." Just in case Aaron didn't realize it, Logan wanted to warn him. "No one gets special treatment or kid gloves. If the goddamn mayor falls under suspicion I'll question him, too. I want the truth for Lyle."

Aaron did smile this time but it wasn't a happy one. This was a cynical, mocking smile that Logan hadn't seen on his former friend before. Time had certainly changed the Brysons.

"I never thought any different. Now…are you going to tell Wade?"

What the hell? Wade probably wouldn't see Logan anyway.

"If he'll talk to me." Logan reached for the front door and then paused. He had one more thing to say. "This isn't over. I'll have more questions about Mary and Lyle. I'll have questions about Lyle's business dealings and his friends. Shit could get ugly so if you know something – anything – it's better to say it now so I can deal with it as discreetly as possible. If Lyle had secrets they won't stay that way for long."

Aaron simply stared back at Logan, a stony expression on his face.

"I don't know anything."

Inwardly chuckling, Logan went back into the house. It looked like it was going to be a rocky road ahead. Nobody wanted to talk and the truth was on a sliding scale. Just another day in Corville.

CHAPTER SEVEN

With nary a backward glance at their parents, Brianna and Colt skipped happily into their grandmother's home, ready to spend the night. Carol had promised them cartoons, popcorn, and ice cream, so clearly junk food was far more important than Mom and Dad.

"Seriously, don't feed them too much sugar," Ava warned, already missing her children. She'd only spent a few nights away from them their entire life. "They'll sleep fine but then get you up in the middle of the night to puke. Especially Colt. He has a delicate tummy."

Logan's reassuring hand settled on her shoulder. "They'll be fine, honey. Your mom's got this."

Carol gave Ava a gentle hug. "Trust me, okay? They've spent the night before and survived. You and Mary turned out pretty good as well."

Ava hadn't meant to imply that her mother wasn't up to the job. "Of course they'll be fine, it's just that I—"

"Worry," Carol finished for her. "That's natural. You can call later and wish them good night if you like. By bedtime, they'll probably be missing you."

Ava wasn't so sure. The twins were at an age now where they were seeking ways to become more independent. Brianna wanted to choose her own clothing every day and Colt just wanted to boss Brianna around. That usually went over like the proverbial lead balloon. Brianna was no pushover.

With one last glance at her mother's home, Ava climbed into the car. They were heading to the park where Lyle was shot. The days in the summer were long and that meant that there was enough sun left to visit the crime scene.

The park wasn't far from her mother's home and they parked as close as they could to the yellow tape surrounding the scene. A deputy sat in his cruiser guarding the area and keeping out the curious.

Logan waved to the officer and the deputy exited his vehicle to shake hands. "It's an honor to meet you, Mr. Wright. You're something of a legend in this town. I'm Deputy Henry Davenport."

Interesting. The one thing the townspeople couldn't say was that Logan sucked at his job. This young man hadn't worked for Logan and Ava had never seen him before. It appeared that the new recruits were getting younger or perhaps she was simply getting older.

"Don't believe half of what you hear," Logan replied, his attention on the scene in front of them. "Drake said that he would keep the scene untouched until I got here. You're taking down the tape after I leave?"

The young man stood up straighter. "Yes, sir. That's my orders, sir."

A smile playing on his lips, Logan nodded. "Thank you, Deputy. I'll let you know if we need anything."

The officer didn't get back into his cruiser, instead leaning a hip against the door and checking his phone. Logan and Ava ducked under the crime scene tape and stood back to survey the scene.

Pulling a diagram from his breast pocket, Logan glanced at it and then pointed to the narrow path. "That's where he was shot."

Shivering at the thought of Lyle dying here alone, Ava trailed after Logan to the exact spot. Standing there she did a three-sixty, looking all around for a likely place for the shooter to hide. In wait.

Assuming of course that Lyle wasn't a random kill. That the shooter had intended to murder Lyle and not just the next person who came along that path.

"There are a few spots he might have hidden," Ava said, studying a clump of trees about twenty yards away. "Maybe there."

"Possibly."

That's what Logan always said when he didn't agree with her but he didn't want to make a big deal out of it. Once the autopsy was complete they'd have a better idea of the angle of the shot but for now they were just conjecturing.

"What are you thinking then?"

Her husband was playing like the Sphinx and not saying much. His expression was blank which wasn't that unusual when he was in thinking mode, but her natural impatience wouldn't allow him to be quiet for long. He needed to talk about what was going on in his head.

"If I were going to kill someone in this park in the early morning hours…"

Logan's voice trailed away, his gaze trained farther up the path.

"If," Ava prompted. "If you were going to do it…?"

He didn't respond, instead striding up the path with her

following behind until he got to a scrub of bushes. Crouching down, Logan hid behind the greenery. "Here. I'd wait for Lyle here. I'd have a clear shot and a good view. Can you go back down the path a ways and see if you can spot me?"

Jogging back to where Lyle was shot, Ava turned and tried to see her husband but couldn't. She ran back as Logan was climbing out of his hiding place.

"In any other season that spot wouldn't have worked. It was all the leaves that covered you." But she couldn't resist pointing it out. "The other spot would work as well, though. He'd have a clear shot from there."

Now Logan was grinning. He loved debating with her.

Who was she kidding? She loved it, too.

"I don't think so." Logan shook his head. "He would have a clear shot but he wouldn't have the best view while he was waiting. Up here he had both."

"But he could also possibly be seen from the road," she pointed out. "Over there he'd be completely hidden."

"And have a terrible view of the path."

They both made good arguments. There was only one way to settle this.

Peeking up at him from under her lashes, she waggled her brows. "Care to make it interesting?"

Stroking his chin, Logan's smile became downright evil. "Perhaps. What did you have in mind, good girl?"

Her heart stuttered in her chest and she drew in a sharp breath. It brought back so many memories of when they were first together.

Good memories. Hot, sweaty ones.

She shrugged, pretending nonchalance. "I dunno. How about a thirty-minute backrub for whichever one of us is right?"

"I'm going to need something better than that."

That had only been her opening salvo.

"A thirty minute backrub…and, well…what do you want?"

That I wouldn't give you willingly and gleefully.

That smile. No one smiled like Logan Wright.

"The backrub and some of your famous lasagna and chocolate mousse."

To anyone listening in, that remark would have sounded completely innocent. Totally G-rated. But Ava knew better. Lasagna always led to a night where they put that chocolate mousse to good use, licking it off each other's bodies.

"Deal. Now what do I get if I win?"

"Anything you want, baby," Logan vowed. "You can name your price."

"So now we wait. In the meantime, have we learned anything here? Other than the shooter likely hid behind those trees."

Chuckling, Logan didn't correct her. "Remember that the sun was barely up. With all this tree and leaf cover, it had to be pretty dark. The shooter either had to know his target or he didn't care."

It was an intriguing hypothesis. "You think there's a chance this could be random? If that's the case, then things in this town could get very bad."

Ava distinctly remembered the D.C. Sniper attacks several years ago. Terror and fear had reigned until the father and son duo were caught.

Logan was staring at the path again where Lyle was shot. "I have no evidence either way. All I have is Aaron swearing that everyone loved Lyle and that no one would have a motive to kill him. If that's true, then it only leaves us with either a random shooting or a case of mistaken identity."

"We have to talk to the jogger who found him. She might be the target."

"She might be the shooter," Logan replied, shoving the diagram back into his pocket. "I want to check her out and make sure she's clean. She's probably just a woman who had terrible luck, but we have to be thorough. No stone unturned."

Was that her husband's way of warning her that he was going to investigate Mary? It hadn't occurred to her that he wouldn't.

"Mary's scared. She wants me to help clear her."

"Good. The spouse is always the first suspect. She'll need all the help she can get, especially as I don't think she's telling us the truth about their marital issues. Her eyes went a little shifty and so did Aaron's when I asked him about it."

"Mary is a total bitch but she's not a killer."

"That's what Aaron said," Logan laughed. "She does have an interesting reputation. But I do want to clear her and get her off my suspects list. I'll have Drake pull all the traffic camera footage around her house so that we can rule her out."

Logan seemed to forget they were in Corville, not Seattle.

"Traffic cameras? Just how many of those do you think they have here?"

"I saw one when we came into town. Let's hope there are more. I've also requested Lyle and Mary's phone records. We need to know who they were talking to these last few weeks or months. You can help me look through those, plus their business and financials."

Ava blew out a breath and rolled her eyes. "You always say you'll help me and then you run off and do something else."

"Nobody combs through files better than you, darlin'. I just slow you down."

"Flattery will get you nowhere."

"I know how to get you sweet," Logan declared with that smug grin. "Now let's get home and get started. We have a lot of work to do."

Another mystery to solve here in Corville, and like the last one it hit close to home. Too close. So many questions and so few answers.

Who would want to kill Lyle Bryson?

It simply couldn't be Mary, and Ava would prove it.

CHAPTER EIGHT

Ava placed the last dish into the dishwasher and pressed the start button. Dinner and dishes were done and the sun was beginning to set low in the sky. Pink, orange, and a dash of purple. She dried her hands on a dishtowel and stepped outside to get a better look and possibly catch a glimpse of her husband. Logan had disappeared after dinner and she'd wanted to give him some time alone.

Time's up.

She knew where he was. That was no secret. And he knew that she knew. He'd climbed into his treehouse to think about the case. And Lyle. And Mary. And the whole being back in Corville thing. He'd come home out of a sense of duty, not because he'd wanted to.

Without conscious thought, Ava found herself walking across the green lawn and straight to the large oak tree. Looking up into the canopy of leaves and branches, she could make out the outline of the treehouse but she couldn't see Logan. Hopefully he wasn't up there with a bottle of tequila like the first time she'd followed him to his treehouse. Or had it been whiskey? She didn't remember anymore, only that she'd been as sick as a dog the next day.

This time, however, she didn't have to shimmy up the tree and take her life into her hands. Logan had installed a very solid and safe spiral staircase that led to a much fancier treehouse than the one he'd had at the ranch. It even had a queen-sized bed that sat right under a skylight where they could lie there and look up at the starry night sky. Before the twins, they'd spent many a night doing just that.

Logan was lying on that bed and staring up at the ceiling, his hands folded behind his head when she found him.

"The sunset is pretty tonight."

She laid down next to him, not pushing him to talk but clearly letting him know she was there if he wanted to. He didn't say anything but he did wrap an arm around her, pulling her closer so her head was resting on his chest. She could feel his heart beating solid and steady underneath her ear. He smelled good. How could one man smell so amazing? She'd never understand it. It was sort of like how he was becoming more handsome and sexy as he grew older. She was just...getting older. It wasn't fair.

It was quite a while later when he finally answered. "Aaron wants me to go see Wade tomorrow and tell him about Lyle."

Ava's first reaction was *hell no*. Her second reaction was *absolutely no*.

"That's...ballsy."

She could feel Logan's chest shake with laughter. "That's one way to put it. He says that Wade has refused to see anyone since the trial, but Aaron thinks he will see me. Gave me some bullshit about how I'm the only one that Wade respects."

Ava sat up and frowned down at her husband. "He tried to kill you."

"That's what I said but Aaron was adamant. He still blames me, by the way, for ruining his life. He said I should have let

Wade go when I realized it was him."

Aaron really did have king-sized balls to say that.

"You should have let go a serial killer just because you had the same father? He actually said that? Asshole."

"He said it." Logan shrugged and shifted on the bed. "I let him know that I didn't take kindly to it. He can hate me all he wants to but this all goes back to Wade. Hell, they didn't have to come back to Corville. That was their choice, not mine."

Lyle and Aaron had moved their families out of Corville for a time, but they had eventually come back once Logan and Ava had moved. They had cited various reasons including business, but Logan had conjectured that they liked the attention. Sure, they hated it too, but they weren't anonymous like they were when they'd moved away.

"You aren't going to do it, are you?"

Even as she said it, she knew what the answer was just by looking at Logan's face. His jaw had that determined set that she'd learned not to argue with. He'd made up his mind and she'd never change it.

"I'm going to, although I'm not sure that Wade will care."

"He seemed to love his brothers."

"Maybe. As much as he was capable of, anyway."

"Then I'll go with you," she offered. "Mom won't mind keeping Brianna and Colt, and they love being with their grandmother."

"No, baby. You're staying here. I'm not taking my wife to a maximum security prison for men. That's crazy talk, woman. Besides, you'd just be waiting around while I talk to him. Better to stay here and get a jump on the evidence. The autopsy should come in tomorrow, plus the ballistic report. We can find out that I was right about where the shot came from."

The one thing she appreciated about Logan was that he

didn't assume that she would stay behind baking pies. He was happy to have her on the investigation as long as she didn't try to do anything *dangerous*. That's when he got pissy and domineering. She'd had to remind him on multiple occasions that she had never been shot at. Logan certainly had and more than once.

"I'm on file duty?" she asked with a heavy sigh. "You get all the interesting assignments."

"I wouldn't call seeing Wade interesting…or maybe I would. I haven't seen or talked to him in years. I would imagine prison has changed him."

Wade had cooperated with authorities to a certain extent, leading them to other victims from years past. There were still some open questions about his college years and Wade was playing a cat and mouse game with the FBI profilers. He kept stringing them along, telling them that there were more bodies out there but then he didn't deliver. Since he was doing life without the possibility of parole, he had plenty of time to play mind games.

"Don't let him get in your head."

Logan tugged her back down, his arm tight around her middle. "Worried about me? I'm not about to let Wade bother me. I'll go there, tell him about Lyle, then come home."

Ava snorted, tossing her hair back and out of her eyes. "Right. He's never going to let it be that simple."

With Wade nothing ever was.

"If he even agrees to see me," Logan replied. "He might not."

"If he doesn't, what then?"

"I'll talk to the prison officials and give them the news. They can tell him. I will have tried and that's all I can do."

There was a part of Ava – a big part – that hoped Wade would refuse to see Logan. A smaller part was curious as to what

Wade was like after all this time.

"Aaron doesn't deserve your help."

Logan gave her a curious look. "What about Mary? Does she deserve my help?"

Good question but the answer wasn't as easy. If one looked at the situation without any sentiment or emotion, the answer was no. Mary had been rather horrible to Logan and her treatment hadn't improved over the years. Logan would have every right to turn his back on Ava's family. But he wasn't like that.

"I don't like to see any innocent person railroaded."

Grinning, Logan picked up a strand of Ava's hair, rubbing it between his fingers. "What a delightful answer. Except it was an answer to some other question, not mine. You seem pretty sure that Mary's not guilty."

"Aren't you?"

"I'm like you. I think your sister is a class A bitch but murder is a bit too far. She'd rather talk behind your back than stick a knife in it."

That was a decent description of Mary Hayworth Bryson.

"Where does that leave us?"

As fast as lightning, Logan rolled over so that he was hovering above Ava. Her pulse kicked into gear and the blood in her veins began to hum with anticipation. They were childless for an entire night. That was something that hadn't happened since…

Hell, she couldn't remember the last time. It had been that long.

"It leaves us right here in this comfy bed. Just you and me. Got any ideas of what we could do with all this free time?"

Ava had several and they all included being naked. Every single one.

CHAPTER NINE

Ava had lost count of the number of times she and Logan had had sex over the years. Not that she'd really been counting in the first place, but in the beginning it had been several times a week. Then after the twins they'd slowed down, although not as much as others might think.

I can't help it. He's just that sexy and good.

Like many couples they'd experimented a bit to keep things spicy. Tried some different positions and even roleplayed, although Ava always felt a little foolish when they did that. There had been flavored lubricants and lingerie for Valentine's Day. There had been padded handcuffs for an anniversary. There had even been a hardback copy of the *Kama Sutra* one year when Logan had come home from a particularly long business trip.

But nothing…not one thing…was as wonderful to Ava as having the weight of her husband on top of her.

They'd tried dozens of other positions and there were many she orgasmed in much more quickly and easily. In fact, Logan on top was one of the hardest for her to climax at all but dammit, there was something about seeing him naked above her, his larger body covering her own that was so freakin' hot.

It was protective. It was sensual. It was mind blowing. It was primal.

Closing her eyes, she lost herself in Logan's kiss as if it was the first time. She hadn't kissed him that night in the treehouse but if she were honest, she'd wanted to. The next day when he'd cared for her so tenderly she'd been lost.

His lips kissed a wet path over her cheek and down her neck, finding that spot he knew sent her over the moon. She moved restlessly against him, lifting her hips and rubbing against his body as her pulse sped up. His cock was hard and pressing against the denim of his blue jeans, wanting to be free. She reached down and pulled his shirt from his waistband and started on his button fly.

Chuckling, he got into the spirit as well, leaning back on his haunches and tugging his shirt over his head before tossing it away. His pants went next and then those talented fingers started in on her garments.

His heady male scent mixed with the aroma of freshly cut grass and the smell of citrusy body wash. She breathed in a lungful as he tossed her bra away, his lips going directly to one rosy nipple while his finger plucked at the other until it was pebbled and tight. His teeth scraped at the sides of the bud before his tongue followed to soothe the small hurt.

"Now, Logan."

Her voice sounded thready and desperate, but then that's what she was. Her body, knowing what pleasure her husband could bring was ready and waiting, and any delay was maddening. She needed him now.

He nipped at her belly, popping open the button of her shorts and slowly pulling the zipper down.

"You're always in such a hurry, baby."

She lifted her head so she could look him in the eye. "You

are such a liar, Logan Wright. You know what I say about lying."

Laughing, he pressed a kiss to her inner thigh that made her wriggle on the mattress. "You always say that if I lie my dick won't get hard, but I must be telling the truth this time."

He dug his hard cock into her leg with a grin and then slid her shorts and panties down, the cotton gliding against her fevered skin.

Tossing them onto the growing pile of clothes, he sat back and surveyed her, his gaze raking from head to toe. At first this had bothered her a little, wondering what he was thinking when he was doing this. But as time had passed, she'd realized Logan was a visual man and the only thing he was thinking was that he wanted to have sex. Specifically with her.

"I'm just in a hurry this time. Not all the time," she said with a hiss as he pressed his lips to the instep of her foot. It was an erogenous zone for her and he knew it, the smug bastard.

Taking his sweet time, he pressed open-mouthed kisses up her leg all the way to the top of her thigh before moving to the other limb and doing it all over again. His five o'clock shadow rasped against her skin sending tingles through her veins. By the time he flicked his tongue over her clit she was a shaking, moaning mess of a woman.

Logan crawled up her body, his cock trapped against her belly as he kissed her deeply, his tongue rubbing playfully against hers. He nudged at her entrance and she reached down to grab his muscled ass, digging her fingers in and urging him to give her what only he could.

He thrust in, his hips snapping forward and she groaned at the sweetness of being impaled so deeply and fully. They knew each other so well, they began their dance as naturally as breathing. Her pelvis swayed side to side with each stroke so that he rubbed her clit with every thrust. As keyed up as she already was it didn't take long until she was teetering on the precipice, ready to tumble over any second.

"Baby, tell me you're close."

His voice sounded like bits of gravel and glass and his soft breath on her shoulder made her tremble as it skidded over her quivering flesh.

"Just…one…more…*yes*."

The last word was said far more loudly than the others and any birds napping in the trees probably flew away in fright, but Ava didn't care as her body shook and pleasure cascaded through her veins leaving her wrung out and limp. Logan reached his peak as well and she watched as she always did, still amazed that this was her man. He was a heap of trouble and a hell of a lot of work, but he was hers to love and care for. She'd never take that for granted.

No matter what happened here in Corville, they were a team. They'd face it together.

CHAPTER TEN

The electronic doors behind Logan clanked shut and the lock engaged loud enough to be heard across the large room. By design, he was sure. There was no doubt that this was a prison. There were at least a half dozen locked doors between him and the outside and a phalanx of armed guards on all sides.

Everything was gray. The tiled floor, the walls, the faces of the guards and prisoners. Depressing and drab, all the hope had been sucked from inside these walls like air from a balloon.

The visitor's room was chilly, over air-conditioned and dry. It smelled of sweat, desperation, and pine-scented cleaner. The pockets of happiness as loved ones reunited weren't enough to lift the blanket of sadness that hung over the institution.

A tall woman in a navy blue suit approached him, her hand held out tentatively.

"Mr. Wright, I'm Dr. Marilyn Bartlett. I'm the psychologist here. May I speak to you, please, before you go in?"

Logan wanted to get this task out of the way as quickly as possible, but it looked like there was one more hurdle to go. Did she talk to every visitor the first time?

"Of course. What can I do for you, Doctor?"

She nodded toward a hallway. "Why don't we speak in my office? I promise this will only take a few minutes."

He followed her into a small office that was as gray as the rest of the institution despite a few personal touches. Even the plant in the corner looked listless and dry as if it didn't want to be here either.

Dr. Bartlett waved him into a chair while she sat down at her desk. Logan was well aware of what that move was. It was a power play. She now had the "power" as the official behind the desk. He'd used it a few times himself. Unfortunately for the good doctor he didn't give a shit about who was the dominant dog in this conversation. He just wanted to tell Wade the news about Lyle and get the fuck out of here.

"It's nice to finally meet you, Mr. Wright. You may not remember me, but I remember you from the trial."

His mind raced back trying to place her but he came up blank. "I'm afraid I don't–"

She shook her head. "Don't worry about not placing me. My hair was different." Her fingers pushed back a stray strand. "I worked for the prosecution during the penalty phase."

Now he knew who she was. Her hair had been different. Much shorter and maybe blonder. She'd also been a spectacular witness for the prosecutor, testifying that Wade Bryson shouldn't receive any leniency because he wasn't capable of it himself. She'd diagnosed him as a sociopath with narcissistic tendencies. He felt no empathy and therefore couldn't feel remorse for his crimes.

"I remember you now. I didn't realize you worked here also."

"I didn't at the time, but I've moved away from private practice." She folded her hands on the desk. "The reason I wanted to speak to you is that Wade Bryson hasn't accepted a visitor in quite a long time, but he's agreed to meet with you. Do you know why that is?"

Logan had a few theories.

"Honestly? I think he wants to mess around in my head for fun."

The woman didn't even crack a smile. Okay, she didn't have much of a sense of humor. So noted.

"You believe that?"

"Yes," Logan answered frankly. "I do. I also think that Wade agreed to see me because he's curious as to why I'm here."

"Why are you here?"

"I'm here to inform him that his brother Lyle was shot and killed two days ago."

Her eyes widened ever so slightly and he could hear her sharp intake of breath, although her features stayed calm and composed.

"I have concerns about that, Mr. Wright. Wade might act out after learning this news. You'll be gone but that will become my problem."

"I would imagine Wade is a problem every day."

The doctor sat back in her chair. "Well…yes. It might be better for me to break the news in a more controlled environment."

"Is there a more controlled environment than a maximum security prison?"

Not a flicker of annoyance or amusement crossed her face. She was like stone. Ballsy woman and she probably had to be to work here.

"I'm concerned about the wellbeing of all the inmates."

Logan wasn't going to push but he was here for a reason. He'd promised Aaron he'd do it and a promise was a promise. Even an unwilling one.

"Are you asking me or telling me that you'd like to break the news yourself?"

"Asking you, of course."

There was no *of course* about it.

"Then I'll do it, if you don't mind."

The doctor merely nodded and stood from her chair. Logan stood as well and followed her to the door that led to the visitor's room.

"Please try and not upset him, Mr. Wright."

"I'll do what I can. It's not my intent to cause trouble."

They had Wade for that.

Logan pushed the door open and stepped into the large room. Along the wall were small cubicles where visitors could sit and visit with a resident. Through a thick piece of plexiglass. Face to face but not really. Logan slowly walked down the length of the room until he found what he was looking for.

Wade.

Settling into a chair across from the half-brother he'd put behind bars, Logan reminded himself not to get caught up in Wade's bullshit. He'd try and play games and get a rise out of Logan.

Not going to happen.

Logan lifted the phone on the wall from its cradle and looked for Wade to do the same. As he'd expected, Wade didn't pick up the receiver right away, instead making Logan wait. A play to establish dominance. If Wade wanted to beat his chest and play king of the jungle from behind bars that was fine with him.

Wade's curiosity though eventually got the better of him and he picked up the phone.

"What a pleasure to see you, brother. This is such a surprise."

It probably was a surprise since Logan hadn't seen Wade in years. The last time he'd spoken to his former childhood friend had been during the trial when he'd been trying to convince Wade to tell about his other victims.

Ignoring the *brother* greeting, Logan wanted to get right to the point. "Aaron asked me to come here today. He says you won't see anyone from the family."

Wade smiled. "I'm seeing you."

It was Wade's mission in life to try and somehow convince Logan that they were alike, one and the same. Brothers in more than paternity.

Logan wasn't buying it.

"There's news about your brother Lyle and I've come here to tell you."

"So tell me."

If Logan had seen even a spark of emotion in Wade's dark, dead eyes he might have tried to softball the news. Soften the blow a little.

But he saw nothing there but a blank gaze. Emotionless and cold. Wade had shown he cared little to nothing for his friends and family. They were there simply to orbit around him, only good for his use or amusement. He acted the part of the devoted big brother but he used those emotions for his own gain. He didn't actually feel anything.

"Lyle is dead." Logan paused for a moment to let the news sink in. "He was shot while jogging in the park. I've been asked back to Corville to help with the investigation."

A corner of Wade's lips turned up. "Always the hero, Logan. You swoop in at the last minute and get the bad guy. Your story never changes."

Neither did Wade's.

"I can see you're heartbroken about your younger brother,"

OLIVIA JAYMES

Logan mocked. "No concern for your family? No questions as to why someone would shoot a seemingly innocent family man?"

"Those are questions for you to answer, my brother. I'm sure you'll find out why and who. After all, you're the great Logan Wright."

"Aaron should have just had the warden tell you the news. I'm wasting my time here."

"What is it you want me to say? That I'm sad? Death is inevitable. You can't cheat it. It's chasing all of us. Some of us just run faster than others."

Death did seem to be chasing Wade. He looked older than before. Far older. His skin was pale from lack of sun and he'd lost weight, making his face appear gaunt and lined. His lips looked thinner and his cheekbones sharper. He was a far cry from the soft, rich businessman he'd been a decade earlier.

"How fast are you running, Wade?"

"Fast enough." Wade stroked his chin and smiled. "I am sad about Lyle. He was a good brother but a stupid man. He didn't understand anything. He wasn't like you and I."

He was at it again. Equating the two of them.

"What do we understand? Enlighten me."

"We understand that it all comes down to power. It's not money or love or friendship or whatever god you pray to. It's power. That's the only thing that matters, and it's the only thing that's mattered for thousands of years. Study history and you'll see."

"You've had a lot of free time to do that?"

Chuckling, Wade sat back in his wooden chair. "That's the thing about prison. You have nothing but time. But you know I'm right because you love power, too. That's why you're a cop, brother. You want power over people like me. You think I'm

64

less than you but we're the same, really. We both want power. We just go about getting it a little differently."

Logan's stomach lurched with nausea at what he was hearing. It was sickening, the way Wade was speaking. He really didn't give a shit about anything or anyone. How had Logan missed the signs all those years? Maybe he simply hadn't wanted to see. Of course, now Wade wasn't trying to hide. He didn't have to camouflage himself and fit in with regular society. He could openly be the monster that he was.

"Did you feel powerful when you took a life?"

That question seemed to snap Wade to attention and he leaned forward, so close to the glass that his breath left a circle of steam. "That's the ultimate power. Like God."

"You think you're like God?"

Wade shook his head. "I know I'm like God. I take life and I can grant it. Just like you, brother. You decide every day who lives and who dies. The ultimate judge."

"I don't." Logan couldn't even fathom what Wade was talking about. "I'm not a cop anymore. I'm just a consultant."

"Yet here you are. Looking for a killer. Why are you here? You hate Corville and the residents hate you. Why did you go back?"

Logan had been asking himself that very question all morning. "I did it for Lyle. He didn't deserve to be shot in cold blood like a dog in the street."

"How do you know?" Wade shot back. "Maybe Lyle was a terrible person. He might have had a secret life that no one knew about. He certainly was weak. He and Aaron are two of the weakest people I know. It's survival of the fittest and they're just cannon fodder."

"They've supported you all these years. They could have cut you off from the family funds but they didn't."

"Only because they wanted to try and save the Bryson family name," Wade argued, shaking his head. "They didn't do it because they loved me. They hate me. They loathe me. No, they did it because they want to believe that there's something to save with the Bryson name."

"And there isn't? You killed to clean up the family."

"I did, but I also knew that there was more than one simple man could handle. Evil runs rampant in the world. Protect your own, brother. It's a cruel life."

Wade was truly delusional if he thought killing innocent people was ridding the world of evil. But then he'd always wanted to be the hero. He'd wanted the adulation of the crowds.

"You sound like a crazy person. Do you listen to yourself anymore?"

Wade threw back his head and laughed, causing several of the guards to place their hands on their weapons and look more alert. "Not only do I listen to myself, I have others that listen to me. I'm something of a celebrity, you know. People follow me around and want just a tidbit of wisdom from me. Women write to me and want to have my babies. They'd do whatever I asked of them. You should see the letters I get. It's really quite amazing."

That was the most disgusting thing Logan had ever heard. Murder groupies. He'd heard about them of course but had never met one. Wade would be in heaven playing in someone's head like that, convincing them of all sorts of horrible things. Manson-like in his influence.

"Since I've delivered the news, I think I'll go. I'd like to say it was nice to see you, Wade, but it wasn't. Not even close."

His statement didn't seem to bother the other man. He was still smiling as if he didn't have a care in the world. That might be true. He certainly didn't have the worries of other people –

jobs, bills, family.

"It was nice to see you, brother. How's that sweet little wife of yours? Ava was always a pretty thing."

Logan didn't like talking to Wade but he liked Wade talking about Ava even less. He didn't even want Wade *thinking* about Ava. But he couldn't show that it bothered him either. Not bothering to reply, he hung up the phone and gave Wade a mock salute before standing. What an incredible fucking waste of time this visit had turned out to be. As predicted, Wade didn't give a shit about Lyle.

He only cared about himself.

CHAPTER ELEVEN

"Jesus, I'm fine."

Logan cracked open the newspaper and buried his nose in it, effectively shutting out Ava's questions. She'd wanted to know how his visit with Wade had gone but he didn't want to talk about it. He was obviously still processing what had happened but Ava was no saint. She was impatient and she wanted to know. He'd barely spoken since he'd returned and she was beginning to worry. Had it been that traumatic?

"Are you sure? Because you ordered onion rings and you hate onions."

They'd decided to get dinner at the local hamburger joint so that neither of them would have to cook. Brianna and Colt were currently coloring in giant dinosaurs on the placemats, one green and the other blue. They'd ordered chicken fingers that they wouldn't eat and fries that they would. The one concession to nutrition was a glass of milk. Ava was a failure as a mother when it came to feeding her children. They were without a doubt the pickiest eaters in the country. Possibly the entire world. Skinny as hell, they barely ate anything at all, so she was just so gosh darn grateful when they did that she wanted to weep half of the time. The other half she just begged them to try a bite. Just a bite.

They rarely did.

"I ordered them for the kids."

"They hate onions too. They hate everything. What's going on? You won't talk to me and that worries me."

Logan glanced at the twins merrily scribbling away. "This isn't a conversation for little ears."

Okay, that made sense.

"Fine. We can talk about it later. How about we discuss what needs to happen next? Where do we go from here?"

"Interviews," Logan answered promptly, folding the newspaper and setting it aside. "Neighbors, friends, coworkers, business associates. Anyone and everyone. I also want to talk to the woman that found the body, too. I want to clear her as a suspect as soon as possible. We also need to interview Mary. For real, this time. But we'll wait to do that until we've combed through their financials and talked to their friends. Then we'll know what to ask. Right now I'd only have general questions."

"Do I get to do any of this?"

"Maybe," Logan conceded. "Although you're most valuable studying those files. Did you see anything today?"

Ava shrugged and sipped her iced tea. "I only have the telephone records so far. They're both addicted to their phones from what I can see. Terrible habit. Anyway, they text all the time and rarely take calls. There are several numbers that they text over and over again, so I think we should ask for those messages. We already have their texts sent to each other and I'll start to go through those next. If they were having marital issues I'm sure it will show up there."

Logan smiled and reached out to ruffle Brianna's curls. "If we're not too tired we can start after the kids go to bed."

Brianna paused her coloring and looked up at her father. "I don't want to go to bed. I want to sleep in the treehouse."

The twins were too young to remember the treehouse but they'd heard stories. Logan had built a much smaller one at their current home, but the entire trip Brianna and Colt had talked about the treehouse as if it was something magical where fairies and wizards lived.

"Not tonight, ladybug," Logan said, dropping a kiss on his daughter's forehead. "We're definitely going to sleep out there one night, all of us, but not tonight."

Colt frowned, looking exactly like Logan when he did. "I want to sleep in the treehouse, too."

"And we will, just not tonight."

"Why not?" Brianna piped up. When she wanted her way, she was a determined child. "Why can't we do it tonight?"

To Logan's credit, he was patient despite the crappy day he'd had. "Because it's going to rain and that means we can't go out on the deck and look at the stars. We need a better night for it."

"So when it doesn't rain, we can sleep in the treehouse?" Colt asked. "What if it never stops raining?"

This was the age for question after question. They could make Ava a little insane but at least this time she could just sit back and let her husband deal with it.

"It won't rain forever," Logan assured his son, but Colt still looked concerned.

"It could. In Seattle it rains all the time."

"This isn't Seattle. It's much drier here."

Colt didn't look happy but Brianna seemed appeased. She reached across and placed her blue crayon on the table and reached for a red one.

"You promise?" Colt asked. "We'll definitely sleep in the treehouse?"

"We definitely will," Logan vowed, crossing his heart with his hand. "We'll play games, and tell ghost stories—"

"I'm not sure about the ghost stories," Ava broke in. "Maybe just games."

"But we have to have ghost stories," Brianna said, signing her name with the bright red crayon. Her masterpiece was complete. "When you camp, you tell ghost stories. I saw it on television."

As far as Ava was concerned, that wasn't the case.

"I think ghost stories can be optional," she replied, keeping her tone neutral. With any luck, the kids wouldn't remember as long as she and Logan kept them busy. They didn't need two scared children who wouldn't fall asleep for the next few weeks. If Logan told a scary story, he could darn well stay up with the kids when they had nightmares.

"Optional ghost stories," Logan said, nodding in agreement but his eyes were twinkling with mischief. Sometimes he was more trouble than the kids. "And popcorn. And pajamas. We'll have so much fun, but not tonight."

Colt scrunched up his nose as he surveyed his green dinosaur. "We had fun at Grandma's house. She made chocolate chip cookies."

Great. More sugar.

"That's good. Grandma makes delicious cookies."

Although Ava's favorite was oatmeal.

"Then Grandpa came over," Colt said, reaching for a yellow crayon. He started coloring the dinosaur feet. "They yelled and then Grandpa left."

Whoa. That was…news. She'd known her parents were having issues, the divorce becoming contentious. But she hadn't thought that they'd be arguing in front of the twins. She'd have to speak to her mother about that. Ava and Logan were very strict about not letting Brianna and Colt hear them raise their voices. It was okay to respectfully disagree and debate, but losing one's temper in front of the twins was a no-no.

"I'm sure Grandpa had something to do." Ava glanced at Logan who wasn't looking happy either. "And you shouldn't listen in to other people's conversations. It's not polite."

Brianna took a drink of her milk, a white mustache appearing above her lip. It was adorable.

"They were loud, Mommy."

His brows raised, Logan shrugged. The kids did have a point.

"Sometimes people get angry but that doesn't mean they don't love each other."

The good Lord knew she'd been pissed off at Logan more than a few times, but she loved him more than she could even comprehend.

Apparently Brianna and Colt were bored with the subject because they started peppering their parents with questions about what they were going to be doing for the rest of the summer. Were they going to stay here with Grandma? Were they going on vacation or back home?

Brianna had been hinting that she wanted to go back to Disney World. Colt wanted to go camping and see bears.

Their meals were placed in front of them and Logan's plate was piled high with onion rings. They'd both ordered the cheeseburger platter. With a sigh, Ava nudged her plate closer to her husband. He'd had a terrible day.

"We can trade if you want."

She'd ordered the french fries, but she could eat the onion rings. They weren't her favorite but she could do it.

Logan didn't get a chance to answer. The bell over the door rang and two older women walked in, smiling and happy, but their smiles immediately fell when they laid eyes on Logan and

Ava.

This is not going to be good.

"Logan—"

He shook his head. "It doesn't matter what they think, babe. Don't engage with them."

One of the women planted her hands on her hips and gave Logan a mean look before stomping across the room to stand in front of their table. Effectively blocked in, there was nowhere to escape unless they wanted to duck down under the booth.

The woman's face had turned an unattractive color of red. "I can't believe you have the nerve to show your face in this town, Logan Wright."

When Logan had first arrested Wade, the good people of Corville had hailed him as a hero. But sadly reality had reared its ugly head. The Bryson family had to sell the business to pay Wade's defense bills. Then people were laid off and the accusing eyes of the town turned on Logan. If he hadn't been so determined to find out the truth, none of it would have happened. The fact that there might be several more dead bodies didn't figure into their calculations. They only knew that they needed someone to blame that wasn't far away in prison. Logan was right there in front of them every day and he looked like a pretty decent target for their frustration, fear, and anger.

Silence stretched between them although Ava could hear the rapid beating of her own heart, pounding in her ears. Her husband was patient and kind. Most of the time.

He lifted an onion ring from his plate and held it up. "Onion ring, Mrs. Walker?"

His genial tone seemed to confuse the woman and she shook her head. "No. No, thank you. Did you hear me?"

He leaned forward this time, close enough that Mrs. Walker wouldn't have any trouble hearing him. His bland expression had turned hard, his features cut from granite. Oh shit. This was not going to go well for the woman. "I did. My children also heard you, so you might want to think about moving along."

A flicker of uncertainty flashed through the older woman's eyes. Logan might be blamed for bringing down the town's biggest employer, but he also had a reputation as a hard but fair lawman. He took no shit. He wasn't going to melt under some old biddy's wrath.

The other woman finally caught up and she took a firm hold of her friend's arm. "Come on, Doreen. Let's just sit down."

Brianna and Colt had finally looked up from their coloring and were watching the exchange with great interest. They didn't know what was happening but even a child could feel the tension in the air and they were curious about it.

Ava twisted in her seat so she was facing both women. The diner had gone eerily quiet as they waited for Logan to respond. But Ava knew him too well. He wasn't going to say anything more. He'd stated his piece and he was done.

"Not in front of my children," she said quietly. "This is neither the time nor the place."

More tugging on Doreen's arm but the woman wasn't ready to give up. "You shouldn't have come back. We don't need you here."

This time Mrs. Walker's friend was successful in dragging her away. Logan visibly relaxed and reached across the table, stealing one of Ava's fries. The children were digging into their own fries and completely ignoring the rest of their food. As usual. If only fries were a vegetable and ice cream a health food.

The hum of conversation in the restaurant eventually picked up again, although Ava could feel the weight of the stares digging into her back.

"I guess the news is around town that we're here," she finally said when the twins' attention was elsewhere.

Logan laughed and a few heads swiveled around at the sound. "Good news travels fast."

"We knew it would be like this."

Logan nodded, taking a bite of his burger. "We did. All this does is make me more determined than ever to find Lyle's killer."

"Then we can go home."

This town wasn't home anymore, and the people weren't her neighbors and friends. This was hostile territory and they'd have their work cut out for them, but they'd find the truth no matter what.

Corville could kiss her ass.

CHAPTER TWELVE

D rake's grim expression perfectly matched Logan's as they trudged to what would hopefully be the last neighbor's home. They'd been questioning the people that lived near Mary and Lyle and so far the story had been the same.

Mary and Lyle argued. Loudly. They'd fight and then Lyle would stomp out of the house and tear down the street, going way too fast. Eventually he'd come back and all would be quiet for days and even weeks. Then the cycle would start all over again.

"I hope Ava is having better luck combing through the phone records," Logan muttered as they knocked on the front door. "Because this is not clearing Mary at all."

"She just might have done it," Drake said, shaking his head wearily. "Statistically speaking, she's our prime suspect."

Logan was well aware of the numbers, but he simply couldn't see his sister-in-law hiding in the bushes and shooting her husband. It didn't mesh with anything that he knew about her. She didn't like to smudge her nail polish, for heaven's sake.

"I doubt most marriages would stand up under the scrutiny," Logan said as the door swung open. An older gentleman,

Howard Styles, stood there unsmiling. But then Logan didn't ever remember Howard cracking a smile in all the years he'd lived in this town. He was, however, a straight shooter and they could count on him to tell the truth.

Drake took the lead since he was the official head lawman in town. "Howard, we were hoping you had a few minutes to chat."

The man nodded and stepped back to let them in. "I've been waiting for you to come talk to me. Saw you across the street and figured you'd get to me eventually so I put some coffee on. How do you take it?"

"Black," Logan replied, following into the kitchen where they sat down at the small round table. "So you know why we're here?"

"I do. What do you want to know?"

Logan accepted the cup of steaming coffee. "What can you tell us about Mary and Lyle? Or more specifically, what can you tell us about Lyle? Habits, schedules, friends. Anything might help us."

Howard considered the question, taking his time before answering. "He was a good guy, friendly and helpful, although he didn't go out of his way to talk to anyone. Mostly he kept to himself, but that wasn't a surprise considering all that had happened with the Bryson family. He would wave and some-times stop and talk for a little while. On Christmas, Mary made cookies and candy and they'd give boxes of it to their neighbors. Good fudge. She'd put green and red sprinkles on it."

Logan didn't really give a shit about the sprinkles but he stayed quiet, hoping Drake would as well. Howard was just getting warmed up. He was the type that had to tell everything single thing he knew, small or large.

"Anyway, Lyle did keep to a schedule. He ran in the park in

the morning pretty much every day unless it was raining or snowing. Even then he'd sometimes go but it wasn't a sure thing. Then he'd go back home and get ready for work. He usually left for the office about eight-forty-five, coffee in hand."

Good details. The person who had waited for Lyle had to have known his habits. Since it was a nice day they'd had reason to believe he would be running that morning.

"You're probably wondering why I know all of this." Howard took a sip of his coffee. "Being retired, I have a lot of time on my hands. Plus, this window in the kitchen looks out over the Bryson yard and driveway."

It did indeed. Howard had a front row seat to the comings and goings.

"Anything else?" Logan asked. Howard had yet to mention the arguments.

"He'd come home about six for dinner, although some nights it was much later. On the weekends, he kept busy with projects around the house and yard. He liked to go to the hardware store."

Drake scribbled in his notebook. "Did they ever have company?"

"Sometimes his brother and the family would come by. Mary had a small book club that met once a week and they'd come over now and then. I'd know because they always blocked my driveway. Not that I really had anywhere to go."

It sounded like Lyle and Mary had kept a low profile. For the hundredth time Logan wondered what had possessed them to move back to Corville where they were the talk of the town and everyone knew their secrets.

"They were homebodies?" Logan asked. "Didn't socialize much?"

Howard frowned. "Well…yes and no. Mary didn't go out

much but Lyle did on occasion. Although I don't know where he was going. He was dressed casually so he could have been heading back to the office. If he left or returned later than nine I wouldn't know about it because that's when I usually hit the hay. But I'm up before the sun every morning and have been for more than sixty years."

As the father of twins, Logan was usually up before the birds and probably would be until the kids were teenagers. Then he'd take great delight in waking their asses up early.

"Anything else?" Drake prompted. "Anything out of the normal routine?"

"Not that I can think of. I'm guessing the other people in the neighborhood told you that the Brysons fought every now and then."

"They argued?" Logan asked, acting as casual as possible. Like this was the first he was hearing of it. "Often or just now and then?"

Howard stared up at the ceiling for a moment. "I wouldn't say a whole lot but every now and then. My sweet Nola and I got in a few shouting matches in our time, God rest her soul. I remember one time I had a few too many at the watering hole and she chased me around the backyard with a rolling pin."

Apparently that was a funny memory for Howard because he was almost smiling. Almost.

"I love a woman with sass, don't you?" Logan could only agree. He did like a woman with spirit. "That Mary never took any guff from Lyle, I can tell you. She'd give him a piece of her mind when he needed it. Of course, women don't chase their husbands around with rolling pins anymore."

Drake nodded in agreement. "I've never had the pleasure but don't give Tori any ideas. She's got a rolling pin the size of a tree branch in that bakery of hers."

Howard refilled their coffees from the carafe on the table. "These days they use a shotgun and they mean business."

About to take another drink of his coffee, Logan froze. What did Howard say?

"A shotgun?"

"Actually, Mary just used a handgun, but Kayla Johnson down the street used a shotgun on her husband when he came home smelling like a whorehouse. The whole neighborhood got a chuckle watching him run back to his car and hide until she calmed down."

Drake and Logan exchanged a glance. This was worth the visit.

"Mary threatened Lyle with a gun?"

Howard shrugged. "Don't know what it was about but she told him to leave and never come back. He did come back, of course, the next day and everything seemed back to normal."

"So it just happened the one time?" Drake asked, his pencil poised over the notebook.

"Far as I know. But it was all peaceful by the next day. Every couple has their own way of working things out."

They certainly did. When Ava was pissed off at Logan she would make frozen waffles for dinner every night until he broke down and asked what the problem was. Then he'd apologize because it was always that he'd done something stupid or thoughtless.

Ava, however, didn't usually brandish a firearm in his direction. Or a rolling pin. Funny how Howard didn't think anything of it. Nola must have been quite a handful back in the day.

They finished their coffee and thanked Howard, waving goodbye as they climbed into the SUV. Drake drove away without saying anything and Logan too was still processing what they'd learned. As they got closer to the station, Logan finally had a few questions.

"Did you know about Mary and Kayla Johnson?"

Drake nodded. "I did know about Kayla because her husband Bill called the cops from inside his vehicle. He was too terrified to leave it until we got there. We took Bill to the drunk tank to sleep it off and told Kayla that threatening people with guns wasn't smart or legal. She'd calmed down at that point so we didn't take her in. Never happened again but then they got divorced a short time later. As for Mary, that's news that she chased him out of their house. You know, this is Montana and everyone has a gun. You've been living in the city for too long, my friend. You wouldn't have batted an eyelash a few years ago."

Perhaps Logan had become too citified. He'd broken up more domestic situations than he cared to remember and they did include firearms from time to time. The fact that Mary waved one in her husband's face wasn't that shocking. What was shocking was that Lyle ended up dead from a gunshot wound.

By trying to clear Mary, he'd only managed to put her further under suspicion. He needed that gun to compare to the bullet they'd pulled out of Lyle. Hopefully Mary would just give it to him so he didn't have to get a warrant.

That would be fun. Have dinner with Ava's family and serve a warrant at the same time.

CHAPTER THIRTEEN

C arol added the dry ingredients to the wet and gave the mix a stir. Ava's mother was making more of her famous chocolate chip cookies but even that wasn't making Mary happy. She'd sulked most of the morning, complaining on and off about Drake, Logan, and the unfairness of the universe in general.

Not that they needed to do any baking, but Ava had a feeling that her mother was simply trying to keep busy. There was something about a death that seemed to bring out the chef in everyone. The refrigerator and freezer were crammed with all of the casseroles and baked goods that had been dropped off by the townspeople.

"They're going to make things sound worse than they really are," Mary pronounced. She wasn't happy that Logan and Drake were questioning the neighbors. In fact, she'd been so upset about it, they'd brought her to Carol's home so she wouldn't have to see what was happening. "They'll exaggerate every little thing."

Ava pinched one of the chocolate chips and popped it into her mouth. The twins loved chocolate chip cookies and were going to be thrilled when they were done with their playdate.

They were spending the morning at Tori and Drake's house playing with their two kids.

"Is there something you don't want Logan and Drake to know? If you don't have anything to hide it's better that they learn all the details."

Mary's lips pressed together. "I don't have anything to hide."

"Then you don't need to worry," Carol replied with a smile. "Let Logan and Drake do their jobs. They said their first task was to clear you. I would think you would be happy about that."

"I don't like people sticking their noses into my personal life."

There was no such thing as privacy when a murder happened.

"They're not pawing through your underwear drawer." Carol's tone was soothing but firm. "They're talking to the neighbors, that's all."

Ava didn't enlighten her mother but that wasn't all. In a box on her kitchen table was phone and financial records that needed looking through. That's where she should be now but she wanted to talk to Carol. In private. So far they hadn't been alone.

"Whose side are you on?"

"Yours, dear, but you're making this harder than it needs to be. You look exhausted. Why don't you go upstairs to my room and lie down for a little while? I'll wake you up when the cookies are done."

To Ava's relief her sister agreed and flew up the stairs. There was always tension when Mary was in the room and in one of her moods. She had a good reason but it was still uncomfortable.

But that meant it was time, so Ava wasn't exactly relaxed.

"Um, Mom…is everything…okay these days?"

Carol poured the chips into the thick batter. "You mean other than my son-in-law being shot to death and my oldest daughter being a suspect? Then yes, things are good. Why do you ask?"

Ava had to concede the question had been stupid. Maybe the direct approach was the best. She took a deep breath and plunged in.

"It's just that Colt and Brianna mentioned that you and Dad argued yesterday."

Carol stopped stirring but she didn't look up, instead bustling over to the corner cabinet to dig out the cookie sheets. "I didn't realize they'd heard us."

"They said you were kind of…loud."

Placing two cookie sheets on the kitchen island, Carol still managed to avoid making eye contact with her daughter. "We had a disagreement."

"So you were just having a little fight?" Ava could have dropped it right then but her mother was being evasive. Did she think no one would notice?

Carol's cheeks had turned red and she took a shuddering breath. "Your father can't seem to decide what he wants and doesn't want in the settlement. Frankly I'm getting tired from all of the back and forth. I just want to be done with it. I want us to have a friendly relationship especially now with all that's going on."

"It's gone on a long time," Ava said. "Maybe you both don't really want the divorce?"

"I know that I want it," Carole sighed, her lips turned down. "Your father and I…I just can't anymore. Ever since he retired his behavior has become more and more erratic. He gets angry at the slightest thing and never seems happy. Least of all with me. I suggested we go to counseling, but he refused and that's when I decided to move out. I've suggested your father sell the house so we can split the proceeds and that's what we argued about. He doesn't want to sell. He doesn't want anything to change. He wants to stick his head in the ground and pretend everything is the same."

Ava digested the information. Like most children – whether grown or not – she didn't like to think of her parents divorcing but it wasn't that much of a shock. They'd had their ups and down over the years. Her father had never been particularly easy to live with either.

"I'm sorry," Ava finally said.

Her mother began dropping cookie batter onto the pans. "I had hoped we could work it out but that's not going to happen. He has to make some changes and he doesn't seem willing to do that."

Bruce seemed to take pride in living in the past. Ava didn't imagine that getting him to change would be all that easy. His favorite decade was the 1950s.

"You could always move in with me and Logan," Ava suggested. Her mother deserved more at this point in her life than being hidden away in this little town. "We're close to the city and there are lots of things to do."

Carol laughed and slipped the pans into the oven. "Just what you and your husband need…your mother underfoot all the time. Maybe you should talk that over with Logan before you offer."

Ava had a feeling Logan would love the idea. He adored her mother – and her cooking – and found her charming whenever she came to visit.

Bruce on the other hand? Not so much. That relationship was strained at best.

"I will talk to him about it. I'm serious, Mom. You should get out, make new friends, and have fun."

"We'll see. Now how about a fresh cup of coffee before you

have to pick up the twins?"

Ava checked her watch. They had about forty-five minutes left and then she had to return back home and get to work on those files. She was positive her sister hadn't shot her husband and that meant someone else did. The truth was always in the minute details. There had to be something there that pointed to the killer. Just one little clue. That's all she needed.

The story was the same when Logan and Drake talked to Lyle's employees. Their boss was a great guy, terrific to work for, but money was tight. Now that he was gone, they were worried about their jobs. Would Mary be closing down the construction company? Logan didn't have the answer but he'd ask.

There was only one more person to talk to. Gary Newhouse, Lyle's supposed best friend according to the people they'd talked to. He was a local real estate agent who was rarely in his office so they met him at the coffee shop in town. Logan and Drake arrived first but Gary came in right after. He looked the part of a successful businessman, dressed in a well-tailored blue suit. His dark hair was cropped close and he wore a big smile despite the fact that his close friend had been gunned down only a few days ago.

Gary shook their hands and sat down at the table after ordering at the counter. "It's nice to see you again, Sheriff. I mean…Logan. Is it okay if I call you Logan?"

"Of course," Logan replied, trying to remember this man but his mind was blank. "I'm afraid I don't remember making your acquaintance the first time."

The real estate agent chuckled and turned pink. "I wouldn't say we actually met so much as we have some of the same friends. I used to hang out at the roadhouse before I was married."

The roadhouse. Logan had taken Ava there a time or two.

"I'm sorry we didn't get to meet then. So thank you for coming to talk to us today. We do appreciate it."

"Anything I can do for law enforcement. I want whomever did this to be caught. My wife is beside herself with fear thinking we have a killer walking the streets of our town." Gary leaned forward and lowered his voice. "Plus, it's bad for business. No one wants to buy a house in a town with a killer."

Drake cleared his throat and coughed a few times. "I would imagine that would be an issue. So we do have a few questions for you. We'd like to talk about Lyle and if he had any enemies. Did he piss off anyone in business? Or perhaps personally?"

Logan was pretty sure he already knew what Gary was going to say but they had to ask no matter what.

"I think everyone liked Lyle, although a lot of people kept their distance. Because of his brother, if you know what I mean."

Yes, Logan knew what he meant.

"But still, he was a good guy. He'd do anything for you."

"So he didn't have any enemies?" Logan asked. "He didn't even cut someone off in traffic?"

Gary smiled and shook his head. "He drove like my grandma so the answer would be no. As for pissing off a business partner, well...not that I know of. He tried to keep his nose clean and do everything above board. The only person that gave him a hard time was Mary, and from what I've seen she gives everyone a rough time. She's a pistol, that's for sure."

Now they were getting somewhere. As the best friend Gary should know more than a casual acquaintance or employee.

"We've heard that he and Mary were having some marital difficulties," Logan replied. "Is that true?"

"It's true." Gary grimaced and looked away. "Lyle had talked divorce a few times but I don't think he was going to do it. He loved Mary but she was tough to live with. Nothing he did was good enough and every now and then it just got to him."

"So what did he do about that?"

Shifting in his chair, Gary wouldn't meet Logan's eyes. "You know...guy stuff. He'd blow off some steam."

"Golf? Shooting range?" Drake queried, scribbling on his notepad. "Maybe having a drink too many?"

A sigh escaped and Gary's shoulders slumped. "Listen, Lyle was my friend and I don't like to speak ill of the dead."

"I'm not asking you to," Logan said, hiding his impatience. "But we do need the truth here. It could be the smallest detail that helps us find out who did this. If Lyle was into something, we need to know about it. You're not being a bad friend. If anything, you're being a good one."

Gary seemed to think about Logan's words. "Lyle...well...Mary could sometimes be rough on him. He'd go have a beer or two and well...there was a woman. He was seeing her off and on. I don't think he was serious about her, though. I mean...I don't think he was in love with her. Not really."

Logan gripped the arm of his chair until his knuckles were white. Lyle had been having an affair. This was a huge revelation.

"Did you ever meet her? Do you know her name?"

"I never met her but her name is Natalie Denning. She's a hairdresser over in Springwood who moonlighted as a waitress a few nights a week at this club he liked to go to. Lyle had a few pictures of her on his phone. She was pretty...and young."

Logan had to ask the next question. "Did Mary know?"

Once again Gary's gaze dropped to the floor. "She did. He said he told her once when they were arguing. Then he promised not to see Natalie again."

Logan and Drake exchanged a cynical glance.

"And did he keep that promise?" Drake asked.

"No. No, he didn't."

CHAPTER FOURTEEN

When Logan had arrived at Mary's house he'd pulled his sister-in-law aside to speak to her about what he and Drake had found out today. Blessedly Bruce had retreated to the living room to watch television and Carol was in the kitchen organizing the massive amounts of food that had been dropped off during the day. At the rate it was appearing, they were all going to have to take some home and put it in their own refrigerators before it went bad.

He'd tried to be delicate when bringing up the subject, but this was Mary. She immediately became defensive and then accused him of deliberately trying to find evidence against her and ignoring all the other suspects.

It was like watching a train wreck in slow motion. He didn't want to look but he couldn't drag his gaze away at the carnage.

"I'm not trying to find evidence against you," Logan explained patiently, shutting the den door behind him so no one else could hear. "If anything, I'm trying to clear you, but the problem is there *are* no other suspects. Every person that I speak with says what a great guy Lyle was and how he had no enemies. The only human being on the planet he fought with was you. Now I find out that you knew Lyle was having an affair and you didn't mention it to me."

"Because it was humiliating." Mary's eyes sparkled with tears. "I didn't want the whole town knowing that Lyle messed around with some bimbo. I want to have some dignity, or are you planning to take that away, too? You've taken everything else from the Bryson family."

He was getting fucking tired of everyone blaming him. He hadn't come back to town to be Mary's whipping boy.

"If your marriage had problems, then you need to look into a mirror. Sadly, I'm not powerful enough to affect your relationship. But if you're looking for your dignity, you might want to speak with Wade. He's the one that went around killing people for fun. I just stopped him."

Red faced, Mary whirled on her heel to face him. "How dare you speak to me like that. Who do you think you are?"

For Ava's sake, Logan had always tried to keep the peace but he was rapidly losing the will to live here. Lyle was a fucking saint to have put up with Mary all these years.

But that doesn't mean she's a killer. She's just a pain in the ass.

"I think I'm the man that's investigating your husband's murder. You do want his killer brought to justice, don't you? Well…don't you? Or are you too worried about your secrets and dignity? Because you may not be able to have both."

Crossing her arms over her chest, she lifted her chin in defiance. "How do you know she didn't kill him? Maybe she was angry that he and I were reconciling."

A woman scorned. It wasn't all that far-fetched, and he'd planned to look into it. He needed to speak with Natalie Denning, preferably soon. Girlfriends often knew the secrets that were kept from the wife.

"I will be questioning her but right now I'm talking to you. How long did you know about Lyle and Natalie?"

Mary rolled her eyes and snorted. "Is that her name? Natalie? Does it end with an 'i' that she dots with a little heart? Jesus, she even sounds immature. Lyle saw her a few times and then he ended it. Case closed."

Apparently, Mary knew the other woman was young. And she didn't like it one bit. Not that Mary was old. She was…around forty, maybe?

Taking a deep breath, Logan held onto his temper. Anger would get him nowhere.

"How long did you know about Lyle and Natalie?" he repeated.

"Six months ago." Mary shrugged and sat down in the brown leather wing backed chair. It looked like one of the same ones that had sat in the library in the Bryson estate. "He told me and then said he was going to end it. He did end it. We were working on our marriage."

"And the night you chased him out of the house with a gun? Was that when he told you?"

Mary's mouth fell open and her face turned a particularly bright shade of purple. Obviously she hadn't expected him to know about that incident.

"We had an argument. All couples do."

Her voice trembled and her hands were at her side, held in tight fists. She probably wanted to smack him.

"You know…Ava and I have had a few fights in our time together but not once have either one of us waved a firearm at the other. What could make a person that angry?"

"He told me about her."

"And you were mad?"

She stood and walked toward the windows, avoiding his gaze. "Who wouldn't be?"

"But he came back?"

"And we worked it out. End of story. It's not nearly as dramatic as you make it sound."

She wasn't getting what was happening here and he was going to have to be the poor bastard that broke it to her.

"I'm not the one making this sound dramatic. Your friends and neighbors are, Mary. They're the ones telling me the stories and if we don't find a way to clear your name, they will be the ones testifying against you at your murder trial. Are you listening to me? Right now, you are the one and only suspect in the shooting of your husband and things are looking bad. You need to start being honest with me or I can't help you."

Shit, now she was crying. He hadn't meant to be hard on her, but she needed to wake the hell up and start seeing the reality of her situation. Nothing was going to protect her. Not the Bryson name and certainly not the reputation she had in Corville. No one would be shocked if she was arrested.

"Do you want to help me?"

"I do," Logan confirmed. "But you better start being more honest with me. Now…is there anything else you haven't told me about your relationship with Lyle? And for fuck's sake, is there anyone else that might have had a motive to kill him?"

Mary slumped against the window frame, more tears dampening her cheeks. "We really were reconciling. I swear it. But things have been rough, especially financially. There never seems to be enough money."

"Now we're making some progress." Logan exhaled slowly, the tension between them lessening, but there would always be some there. She didn't like him. "How about we start at the beginning? When you and Lyle moved away from Corville. Tell me about that."

Maybe the shooter was someone from Lyle's past. Logan had to look at every angle if he was going to clear Mary, but she was going to have to tell him the truth. No more surprises.

CHAPTER FIFTEEN

Later that evening, Ava kissed Colt and Brianna goodnight before joining Logan in the kitchen. Boxes of documents had been delivered during the day and despite her best efforts she had yet to break the seal on even one of them.

He slid the frozen pizza onto the oven rack before turning and giving her a quick kiss on the lips. "Are they asleep?"

"Do you hear that?"

Frowning, he stopped and listened. "I don't hear anything."

Ah, the blessed quiet. Some days Ava couldn't even pee without two kids pounding on the bathroom door wanting in.

"Exactly. They're asleep and they should stay that way." She picked up the cardboard box on the counter. "Frozen pizza? Did we have this in the freezer? I could have made a homemade pizza if you had a craving."

The twins had eaten dinner earlier. Chicken nuggets and applesauce. Colt had nibbled a piece of broccoli but Brianna had turned up her nose in disgust.

Plucking the box out of her hand and tossing it into the trash, he gave a mock sigh. "I stopped at the store. Am I the only romantic soul in this marriage? You really don't remember?"

She really didn't. What was he talking about?

"Mea culpa. You're the king of romance. Now will you tell me what frozen pizza has to do with romance? I think I missed it."

"I fixed us a frozen pizza that first night that we worked together on the case," he explained. "Just like tonight."

Smacking her forehead, she groaned. "You're absolutely right. I'd forgotten. You really are the king of romance. That's so sweet that you remembered. You're not going to let me forget this, are you?"

"After you busted my balls about Valentine's Day? Let's just say we're even."

She'd given him a hard time when he couldn't get home to celebrate Valentine's Day. Again. And his over the top flowers and chocolate a few days later hadn't softened her mood at all. He'd promised to be home and then he wasn't. It was becoming all too frequent.

He'd been with Kim working on a case.

She didn't remind him that they'd been planning on going out on Valentine's Day for weeks. That she'd made reservations at a romantic restaurant and bought a new outfit. She also didn't remind him that Misty and Jared had volunteered to watch the twins that night. He'd had a good excuse, after all. They needed to catch the bad guy and they had done exactly that the next day.

Sometimes it was simply hard to be apart.

Ava knew that Valentine's Day was just a made-up holiday designed by corporate America to separate people from their money and guilt men into buying flowers for their wives once a year, but that didn't stop her from wanting him with her on that day. It didn't stop her from feeling the loneliness as his business trips seemed to drag on longer and longer with each assignment.

Logan was a great lawman and this was part and parcel of his world. But she still missed him. A hell of alot.

It was a good idea to change the subject. "Are we going to look through these papers after dinner?"

"I was hoping," Logan replied, checking his phone and then plugging it into the charger. "After what Drake and I dug up about your sister and Lyle today, we need to find some evidence that points in another direction."

After he'd explained what he'd learned, Ava was worried about Mary. Her sister had a temper and although Ava didn't think she would shoot someone, other people might. Jurors especially.

Starving, they wolfed down the sausage pizza and then settled onto the living room floor. Boxes were stacked around them and Ava wasn't sure where to begin. Should she continue on with the phone records or make a start on the financials?

Logan answered without her having to ask. He picked up a huge box from the top of the pile and dropped it next to her. "How about you dig into those financial records and I'll pick up Lyle's text messages?"

Ava lifted the lid on the box. "Sounds good."

They were both quiet for the next hour or so, the only sound the soft murmurs from the television set. Ava didn't even know what was playing but she often kept it on just for the background noise when she was working.

Setting aside the last bank statement, Ava groaned and rubbed at her lower back. It ached from the position she'd been sitting in and her knees were stiff as well. She needed to exercise more but there never seemed to be any time.

Honestly, what she'd found in the stack of papers wasn't making her day any better. If anything, it was far worse than she'd imagined. She'd kept digging through the documents hoping to find something to mitigate the damage but instead she'd found a life insurance policy.

On Lyle. With Mary as the beneficiary. She didn't have money problems any longer.

"Find anything?" Logan asked, reaching around to knead her shoulders. Ava sighed with pleasure as his strong fingers worked on a particularly large knot at the base of her skull. "Jesus, woman, your shoulders and neck are like concrete."

"Writing is hard on the body. I'm way past due for an adjustment and massage."

"We'll get the heating pad out." His hand skated over her neck and lifted her hair out of the way. "Lyle was definitely having an affair. I read the texts."

"Did he stop like Mary said he did?"

She still couldn't believe that Mary had chased Lyle out of his own home with a gun.

"No. Well, maybe. The texts seemed to slow down about a month ago but they didn't stop. At least the sexting ceased, though. That's shit you don't want to read, let me tell you."

She was grateful that Logan had offered to take the phone records. She hadn't been looking forward to reading private communications between Lyle and her sister. Or his girlfriend. People didn't seem to realize that they had little privacy on their phones or on the internet.

"He sexted with her? Ick."

"I'm going to need some brain bleach. There are things I know about his kinks that I didn't want to know. I mean, more power to him and all but damn…I sure as hell wouldn't want people knowing what I like in the sack. No eye contact with Mary next time I see her."

Ava didn't want to think about her sister's sex life. At all. Never.

"Stop talking about sex," Ava groaned again. "I'm going to need brain bleach, too. You need to take whatever you read to the grave."

"But I want to share everything with you, pumpkin."

"If I can't share childbirth then you can't share this."

Logan laughed, his fingers digging into an especially sensitive spot that had her sighing in bliss. "If I remember correctly, you pointed to me and ordered the doctor to cut off my balls. I think you *shared* plenty."

"I birthed twins, Logan. Twins. With no epidural."

Not on purpose, though. She'd wanted pain medication but by the time they'd arrived at the hospital the doctor had informed her it was too late. She was too far gone and she was going to have to do this the old-fashioned way. Then after pushing for what felt like forever, the doctor had ended up doing a c-section.

"How about we change the subject and talk about what I found?" Ava said sweetly, holding up a piece of paper. "Lyle and Mary were basically broke. They lived on credit and were robbing Peter to pay Paul. But this caught my eye."

Logan took the document and perused it. "Lyle had life insurance and Mary was the beneficiary. A half million is a whole lot of motive."

"It's a huge policy for a couple with no children and barely any money," Ava observed. She and Logan had gone through the 'how much life insurance do we need' dance when Colt and Brianna were born. "They could barely pay their car lease but they never missed a payment on the policy."

Logan rubbed at his eyes and set the document back into the box. "This is bad. Very bad. I'm going to have to tell Drake tomorrow. We need to find that girlfriend and talk to her. If Lyle did actually end their relationship, that might be a motive for murder and we'd finally have another suspect."

"And if he didn't?"

"Then your sister better hire a good attorney."

CHAPTER SIXTEEN

"I asked Jared to check out the girlfriend," Logan said in a whisper as he watched the mourners file out of the church. It was Lyle's funeral and the whole town appeared to have shown up to pay their respects. Or get a good look at the possible murderer – Mary.

Or perhaps to give Ava and Logan dirty looks. That seemed to be the favorite pastime of many townsfolk. To their credit, they weren't bothering to hide their disdain. At least they were honest. Logan respected that.

Drake craned his neck to see Mary who was standing at the front of the church by the coffin, looking sad and devastated. She'd sobbed through the entire eulogy and then some.

"Should I arrest her? With the life insurance policy and all she had motive."

Logan shook his head. "No, not yet. We're still in the early stages of the investigation and we don't want to tip our hand. Besides, she's not a flight risk. We know where she is and what she's doing pretty much every minute of the day thanks to Corville's gossip mill. She's not going anywhere."

And hopefully that life insurance policy was simply a terrible coincidence. He didn't want to see his sister in law arrested.

"What if Jared can't find the girlfriend?"

"He'll find her," Logan replied with confidence. "Wherever she's hiding, he'll find her. It just takes time."

Drake had sent a deputy to the girlfriend's residence this morning but it was empty. A neighbor had said that the woman had been seen loading a suitcase into the trunk of her car and driving away.

She was on the run. The question was why. Guilty conscience or just scared?

Drake eyed the stream of people as they exited the church. "Do you think someone local did it?"

"I know you're hoping that it's some random stranger but that's a rarity. People generally aren't killed by strangers. I wish I had better news for you. It's probably a Corville resident. You're going to be as popular as I am when this is all over. If you're smart, you'll blame it all on me. After all, you have to live and work in this town."

"They're just being stubborn." Drake shook his head sadly. "There is no way they didn't want you to catch a killer. They were screaming about the vigilante killer and how he needed to be stopped but the minute it was someone who employed a third of the town, they weren't so upset any more. Acting like a bunch of children, if you ask me."

Logan felt the same way but he didn't often express his frustration. The situation was out of his control. He just didn't like that Ava was guilty by association. She didn't deserve their shit. All she'd been doing was learning how to investigate so she could be a better writer. He'd been the one that had arrested Wade and put him in prison.

Speaking of his lovely wife…she was trapped next to her sister, mother, and father. Bruce Hayworth was waving his arms animatedly and probably speaking loudly – although Logan couldn't hear him. It was simply that Bruce always spoke a little too loudly. He seemed to think that everything he said was important.

"Time to rescue Ava," Logan said. "Just give me a minute and I'll be right back."

Drake's eyes were wide and he backed toward the door. "Good luck, man. I'll be waiting outside."

Logan would need all of that luck and more. He wasn't exactly popular with his father-in-law and he'd already had a lecture from the older man about how Logan's profession was going to get him killed at a young age. Logan hadn't bothered to remind Bruce that Lyle had a boring desk job and had managed to get himself dead without a badge. Besides, people rarely pointed a gun at Logan anymore. With his new position at the consulting firm, it would be considerably less. He'd be home more, too. At least that was the plan.

Striding down the aisle between the pews, he didn't give any of the stragglers a glance, his gaze trained on his beautiful wife. Her face was red and tearstained and she kept dabbing at her eyes with a tissue. The service had been a lovely tribute to a good and kind man. Hell, even Logan had been choked up at one point. No one deserved to go out the way Lyle had.

"Ava, are you ready to go? We need to check on the kids."

Drake's wife had helpfully offered to watch Colt and Brianna today along with her own children. Both Logan and Ava agreed that they were too young to really understand what was going on and they hadn't spent much time with Mary and Lyle. Plus, they both hated to have their children witness the stares and whispers from the people around them.

"You're coming to the house, aren't you?" Carol asked anxiously, her arm around her weeping daughter. "Everyone will be there."

That was why Logan didn't want to go but he couldn't think of a good excuse. It was expected and it was polite, so he would be there whether the lovely citizens of Corville wanted him to be or not.

"Of course we will, Mom," Ava said, giving her mother a hug and then a kiss on the cheek. "We just need to check on the kids first, and then we'll be there."

"Just bring them." Bruce's voice boomed and bounced around the now empty church. "They should be with family today."

"Dad, they're six."

"No better time to learn about the circle of life."

Logan was of the opinion that they could learn about the circle of life with a hamster or a guinea pig and save the humans for a later date.

Placing an arm around Ava, he urged her toward the door. "Well, we'll see you at the house. Send a text if you need us to stop anywhere or pick up something."

They hurried up the aisle and out of the church where Drake was leaning against the SUV and talking on the phone. Logan pointed to his car and waved to his friend as he helped Ava into the passenger seat. He slid behind the wheel and started the vehicle.

"I talked Drake out of arresting Mary."

Ava's head jerked around, her mouth hanging open. "Is that an option? I mean…we've barely started here."

"That's what I told him." Logan pulled out into traffic. "He was fine with it. We really need to talk to that girlfriend. We need to know what she knows."

"Hopefully Jared can find her."

Logan grinned at the thought of his friend and partner not

being able to track down their person of interest. "He'll find her. He always does. How did I do back there?"

He'd tried to be sensitive and supportive of Mary even though they didn't get along. She might not be nice to him but she was still a widow burying her husband today. He wasn't unsympathetic.

Unless she had shot Lyle, of course. But he really honestly didn't think she was the one. It didn't fit her personality. Everything he knew about her didn't point to killer.

"You did fine," Ava assured him. "Even Daddy was impressed."

Snorting, Logan didn't believe that for a second. "Bullshit, baby. He hates my guts more than ever. I'm a continual reminder that the big bad womanizing sheriff defiled his baby girl. He'll never forgive me for that one."

"He liked Lyle."

"It's not the same and you know it. Lyle was a pillar of the community."

Ava rolled her eyes. "You were the sheriff. It doesn't get more pillar-like than that."

"My job meant getting my hands dirty," Logan replied in a mocking tone. "Lyle got to push paper from one side of his desk to the other. Very different. But at least your mom likes me."

The corners of Ava's lips turned down. "They're definitely getting a divorce."

Reaching for her hand, he gave it a reassuring squeeze. "Hey, one family problem at a time, okay? They might work this all out."

Though he doubted it. Bruce had become increasingly difficult these last few years. Angrier and quick to temper. Poor Carol was at the end of her rope, frankly. How she'd put up with it for so many years Logan had no idea.

"Somehow I don't think they will." Ava's voice was soft and a little trembly. "If I ask you a question will you answer me honestly?"

He already knew what she was going to ask.

"Always."

"Do you think she did it?"

"No," he answered with no hesitation. "I don't. But we have to keep an open mind and look at all the angles. We have to eliminate Mary as a suspect, and the first step to doing that is to talk to the girlfriend."

"But Jared has to find her first."

As if on cue, Logan's phone chirped in his pocket. "I bet that's him. He might have found her already."

They were due for some good news.

CHAPTER SEVENTEEN

L ogan had dropped Ava off at her sister's house and then he and Drake headed straight for Springwood. Natalie Denning had a close friend who lived there and according to Jared she had just in the last hour posted a photo of the two of them together on social media. If she was trying to keep a low profile she wasn't doing a great job of it.

"Ava's mad," Drake stated as they pulled onto the street where Natalie was hopefully staying. It was a quiet residential neighborhood with almost identical beige townhouses all lined up like soldiers.

"She is but she understands that she can't always go along. She's not a cop and she can't visit a person of interest and ask questions. Now if we bring Ms. Denning into the station and ask her questions there, Ava can watch on the monitor."

He was definitely going to get the third degree when he returned home, though. Ava was going to want every little detail, right down to Natalie's expressions and body language.

"I don't like pissing off my wife," Drake laughed. "She won't bake any of my favorites when she's mad."

Drake's wife owned the bakery in town and somehow he

hadn't managed to put on thirty pounds since marrying her.

"I don't like it either, but luckily Ava doesn't like to cook."

She had other far more effective ways of torturing Logan.

Logan stopped the vehicle a few doors down from their destination. Picking up his notes, he checked the make and model of Natalie Denning's car against the one parked in front of the house. "Blue Chevy Malibu. That's probably her."

"How do you want to do this?" Drake asked. "Go in as friends? Be all sympathetic? Or big, bad cops? Scare her a little? We could be one of each."

"Let's go the friendly and sincere route. I think we'll get further with that. We don't know if she even knows anything so let's tread lightly here. I want her to voluntarily cooperate if possible. If she gets nasty or tries to run? Then all bets are off. Take her back to the station and question her. Make it official and serious."

Logan parked the car and climbed out of the SUV, taking a peek into Natalie's vehicle as they walked up to the door. Nothing looked unusual or out of place. In fact, it was neat as a pin. Not so much as a half empty water bottle or gum wrapper. Nothing that said *I'm a killer on the run from the law.*

Drake knocked on the door and Logan stood back a ways, wanting to study how Natalie reacted to her uninvited visitors. The door swung open and a pretty blonde stood there, her gaze running back and forth from Drake to Logan.

"Can I help you?"

The woman's voice came out squeaky and nervous, her fingers gripping the doorframe tightly enough to turn her knuckles white.

Drake tipped his hat and smiled. "Ma'am, I'm Sheriff Drake James from Corville and this is my consultant Logan Wright. We were hoping to speak to Natalie Denning today. We have a few questions for her."

Shifting on her feet, the blonde looked over her shoulder before answering. "Natalie isn't here. I don't know where she is."

Logan didn't like it when people lied. He'd been lied to his whole life, so it was a sore spot with him. Especially as this same woman had posted a photo on Instagram not an hour ago. The background in the picture looked a hell of a lot like the living room couch that Logan was currently staring at.

As patiently as possible, Logan pulled his phone from his pocket and held it up for the woman's inspection.

"Is this you, Miss Ludlum? You are Dani Ludlum, correct? And you posted this photo about 90 minutes ago?"

Red crawled up Dani Ludlum's cheeks. "I did. I mean...I did post that but it was a picture taken about a week ago."

Plausible. But not probable.

Logan pointed to the car in front of the house. "And did Miss Denning leave her automobile with you as well?"

Dani Ludlum nodded vigorously. "Yes, that's exactly what she did. She's...out of town...on vacation. I don't know when she'll be back."

"Kind of an open-ended vacation," Drake replied, pulling out his small notebook from his breast pocket. "Would you mind if we left her a note? You can give it to her when she gets back."

"She really needed to get away." Dani cast another glance over her shoulder. "I guess I could give her a message."

"You know, ma'am," Logan said, his gaze trained at where Dani kept looking, waiting for some movement. Natalie Denning was inside listening to this entire conversation. "I think you need the vacation more. You seem awfully nervous and tense."

Dani's read face turned pale and she gripped the doorway even more tightly. "I'm not used to talking to the police."

Logan gave her his best charming smile. Once upon a time, it had worked on a myriad of females. Now he kept it only to get his wife out of bad moods.

And moments like this when he needed to get someone to talk.

"We're harmless," he assured the woman. "We just need to talk to your friend. Where did she go on vacation? The tropics? I've always wanted to visit Hawaii."

Drake finished writing the note and ripped off the paper from the pad. "Here you go. My phone number is on there. She can call me anytime, day or night."

"Thank you," Dani said, looking at the paper and then folding it in half. "I'll give it to her when she gets back."

Logan wasn't done. She hadn't answered the question. "You didn't say where she went."

Dani opened her mouth but the words didn't come. It took a few tries but she eventually seemed to find the answer. "Florida. She's visiting Disney–"

"Forget it, Dani." A female voice came from behind the blonde. "They know I'm here. I can tell."

Of course I knew. You ladies aren't Butch and Sundance. You parked your car in front of the house and posted to social media.

The voice had a form and a woman stepped out from behind the hallway wall. Tall and slender, Natalie had chocolate brown hair that hung down her back and just touched the waistband of her faded blue jeans. She was younger than Logan had envisioned, although he wasn't an expert in women's ages. She looked to be about twenty-five or so but it might simply be her casual dress and bare feet.

"Miss Denning?" Logan took a step forward trying to meet

her gaze. He wanted her to know that he was someone she could trust. "We just want to speak with you."

There was a moment that he thought she might turn and run – she looked like she wanted to – but then she finally nodded, motioning them inside. This was progress. Now he just had to get her to talk.

The young woman shook visibly and Logan tried to calm her down. He wasn't here to accuse her of anything. He simply wanted some answers.

Now...if she said something incriminating...that was a different story. She might have a motive to kill Lyle but she wasn't alone.

"Natalie, why don't we sit down and you can tell us about your relationship with Lyle Bryson," Logan suggested. "I meant it when I said that we're just here to talk to you."

Swallowing hard, Natalie sat down on the couch with her friend Dani right next to her, holding her hand. Logan took up residence on the loveseat with Drake perched on the ottoman at the far corner of the coffee table.

Natalie took a shaky breath. "I'm not sure what you want to know."

Logan wasn't sure either. He had many questions but some might not be important based on the answers to others.

"Why don't we just start at the beginning? How did you meet Lyle?"

Her lips turned up at the corners as she began her story. "I know this is going to sound cheesy but we met in line at a fast food place. We were both there for lunch and it was really busy. We chatted and then we ended up sharing a table because there weren't many places to sit. He was such a gentleman and he really listened."

Hating himself, Logan still had to ask it. "Did you know he was married when you met him?"

Shaking her head, a few tears streaked down her pale cheeks. "I swear I didn't. He wasn't wearing a ring and I know that because I checked. We're always saying that the good ones are married so I looked."

"But you eventually found out?"

"Yes, I guess it was our third or fourth date. He said that he was married but they were separated. He said they hadn't been happy for a long time and that they had grown apart. He said they were getting a divorce."

The only thing missing was Lyle telling her that his wife *didn't understand him.*

"Mary says that they reconciled and that Lyle ended things with you."

That seemed to surprise Natalie. Her brows flew up and her mouth fell open.

"That's a lie. Lyle never ended things with me. He was going forward with the divorce. I saw the papers in his briefcase."

If there were papers, then there was an attorney. Logan needed to find out who that was.

"Do you know the name of his divorce lawyer by any chance? I'd like to speak with him as well."

Brows pinched together, Natalie at first shook her head but then nodded. "Marshall. The last name was Marshall. I don't remember the first name, though."

That would be Brent Marshall. He was a local attorney who handled mostly civil cases. Logan knew exactly where to find him.

"That's great, Natalie. I know who you're talking about. Now let's talk a little more about you and Lyle. It seems like you and he didn't communicate as much the last few months. Much less than before."

"That's true. Lyle was crazy busy doing some business deals and he didn't have a lot of free time."

I want to know all about those business deals.

"What kind of business deals?"

The young woman's face turned red and she didn't answer right away. Her friend Dani whispered something in her ear and Natalie shook her head, not liking what she was hearing.

"I can see you don't want to tell me about them, but it's okay. Lyle doesn't expect you to keep any secrets now. He needs you to be honest so we can find his killer."

A fresh spate of tears fell on Natalie's face and she reached up to dash them away with her fingers. "You don't understand. You couldn't possibly understand."

Leaning forward, he gave her his most encouraging smile. He wanted to be as calm and confident as possible. "I've been in law enforcement for a long time, Ms. Denning. I've pretty much heard it all. I doubt you can shock me."

"Lyle owed money. Lots of money. And to dangerous people."

CHAPTER EIGHTEEN

L ogan had assured the young woman that he couldn't be
shocked and he wasn't. However he was surprised. Not
that Lyle owed money. Since Wade's arrest, the Bryson family
had plenty of cash flow issues. No, he was surprised to hear that
Lyle owed money to people Natalie deemed dangerous. A
straight arrow, Lyle was a rule follower and always had been.
Hell, he didn't even cross the street when the light said *Do Not
Walk.*

"Dangerous?" Drake had been quiet up to now but he'd be
very interested in the criminal element in his town. "How do you
mean...dangerous? Did you meet any of these people?"

Sighing, Natalie's shoulders slumped and Dani put her arm
around her friend in support.

"Yes, I've met them because I'm the one that introduced
him. They're my employers. Or...my ex-employers. I'm afraid to
go to work. I take a few shifts a week as a waitress there."

If Logan hadn't been paying attention before, she had all of
it now. This was becoming quite the tale.

"Where do you work?"

"The nightclub out by the highway near Springwood. The

Bell Tower. It's just a part time thing. You know...for extra money." She hesitated, her gaze skittering over to Drake and then back to Logan before continuing. "There's more there than just a nightclub, though."

Drake's jaw tightened and he nodded in agreement. "We've suspected for some time that illegal activity was going on there, Ms. Denning."

Raising an eyebrow, Logan gave his former deputy a questioning look. *Illegal activity* was rather vague.

"Gambling, prostitution, and drugs," Drake said with a grim smile. "The law enforcement trifecta. There's probably some money laundering going on there, too. Tanner spoke about it at our last couple of meetings."

"I don't know about any drugs or prostitution," Natalie protested, indignation in her tone. "I've never seen any of that. I've only seen...the gambling room upstairs."

Natalie's gaze had fallen to the floor and Dani was whispering urgently in her ear. The young woman kept shaking her head no.

"You have to tell them," the friend said, jumping up from the sofa. "They'll find out eventually."

Sniffling, Natalie finally agreed. "It's just...it's all my fault. If I hadn't introduced Lyle to my boss, none of this would have happened."

Logan was beginning to put the puzzle together in his brain, filling in the blanks with ideas of his own, but this young woman needed to confirm the story.

"Lyle came to the nightclub," Logan said. "He came to see you."

"Yes, he'd come and have a drink and we'd talk on my breaks."

"Then you introduced him to your manager. That's a pretty

normal thing to do."

Natalie dragged the back of her knuckles across her damp cheeks. "Cory, my boss, invited Lyle up to the gambling room."

Shit. Logan knew what was coming next.

"Lyle lost money there, didn't he? A lot of it."

She nodded, taking a shaky breath. "At first it wasn't too bad. He'd win some and he'd lose some. But then it seemed to get worse and he'd come in several times a week and his losses kept piling up. You can't owe people like Cory money and not pay it back."

No, you can't. And Lyle should have known better.

"And you think Cory shot Lyle because of the debt?"

"I bet he had one of his goons do it. He wouldn't do it himself."

The theory made sense. Except…

If this Cory killed Lyle he wasn't ever getting the money back. Drake had to be thinking the same thing based on his dubious expression. Usually they broke both of your legs and threatened your family. Death was pretty final unless Cory had written off the debt, which would be insane because the Bryson's might not have cash, but they did have assets. Equipment, land, real estate. There was money to be had if they were patient enough.

"And you think you might be next?" Drake asked. "You think your life is in danger?"

Natalie threw up her arms, two red flags coloring her otherwise pale face. "I'm practically a witness. I know that Cory has motive, so of course he's going to come after me. I'm terrified to go to work or my own home."

Since Logan didn't know if Cory had Lyle shot or not, he couldn't make a determination as to whether Natalie Denning was in danger. It was a possibility that they needed to take into account.

"Then you probably shouldn't be posting photos of the two of you on social media or parking your car in front of the house," Drake observed. "Maybe you really should go on a vacation."

Logan was already texting Jason to see if they could get one of the trainees out here to babysit the women until he'd closed this case. He didn't want to take any chances and he absolutely didn't want to send Natalie out of town. He was afraid he'd never see her again. He hadn't confirmed her story and this could all be a load of horse shit. She might be guilty as hell despite all the angst and tears.

Damn, I'm getting cynical in my old age.

His phone dinged with a confirmation. The consulting firm would provide the two young women with protection. But not here. They'd go to a more secure location.

"I'm talking with my partners about a safer option," Logan replied. "But you'll have to leave this house. Anyone can find you here."

Dani and Natalie exchanged a glance, and then Dani spoke. "I can't leave my job, but I think Nat should go."

Logan already didn't like it. "I can't protect you here."

The young woman shrugged. "I know but I can't lose my job."

Logan sighed and began tapping out a new text. This time to a friend. "Let me get in touch with Sheriff Tanner. Maybe he can have a patrol come by several times a day."

Just the mention of Tanner Marks had Dani smiling. "He's such a good man. His wife is so pretty, too. And their little girl is adorable."

Amanda Marks was incredibly cute. She looked a lot like her mother Madison, thank heavens. Tanner wouldn't be an attractive female.

"We'll work something out," Logan promised. "In the meantime, I need to know every detail about Lyle's gambling. What he liked to bet on, how much he lost. I also want everything you know about Cory and his business partners. Can you do that for me, Natalie?"

"I can but I'm not sure that I know all that much."

"You know more than you think you do," he assured her. "Sometimes the littlest thing is the most important."

Ava was going to be pissed as hell that she'd missed this. Maybe he should pick up dinner on his way home.

On the bright side, Mary wasn't their best suspect anymore.

Ava hadn't had a great day with her sister and her evening wasn't getting any better. Her loving husband Logan had just informed her that she was sitting out another part of the investigation. Again. This was becoming a habit.

"It's too dangerous," Logan said flatly, his lips in a firm line. She knew that look and it didn't bode well for changing his mind. When Logan Wright decided something, it took damn near a zombie apocalypse to change his mind. "You could get hurt or killed. We don't know what this Cory is up to yet. He could be a killer or just a small time thug, but either way you aren't going to be there. You can wait in the police van across the street and listen in, but that's as close as you're getting."

He made a good argument and she couldn't really refute any of it, but there was something he hadn't considered.

"Having a woman with you will make you seem much less of a threat," Ava said. "You'll be perceived as harmless. If you're alone or with Tanner, they'll be much more suspicious. Tanner, what do you think?"

The subject of their discussion was sitting at their kitchen table drinking a cup of coffee. Holding his hands up in a sign of surrender, he laughed. "Don't drag me into a marital disagreement. I'm like Switzerland here. Completely neutral."

"You'd take Madison into an undercover operation?" Logan queried, his brows almost to his hairline. "I don't believe that for a moment."

"No, I wouldn't," the older lawman conceded with a grin. "But what we do shouldn't have any bearing on what you do. Switzerland, remember?"

"But don't you think having a woman there will make them less suspicious?" Ava argued. "I can be useful in this investigation."

Her handsome husband scowled at her statement. "You are useful. But you don't go in the field. End of story. Decision made. You are right, though, we would be perceived as less of a threat with a woman. That's why I've asked Jason to send Kim. She and I can pretend to be a couple. Obviously Tanner can't go in there. They know he's the sheriff."

Kim. Logan and Kim were going to pretend to be a couple. She didn't like the sound of that at all. In fact, how many times had they already done that? They were spending far too much time together and now good ol' Kim was coming to save the day. As if there were no females for hundreds of miles around Corville. Logan had to import his lovely partner.

"You're bringing Kim in."

"She's a trained law enforcement officer," Logan pointed out. "It only makes sense. I'm not going to send my wife and mother of my children into an unknown situation. Not going to happen, babe."

Kim was trained and could handle herself. She and Logan had far more in common than Ava and Logan did.

My husband is not cheating on me. He loves me and the children. He loves his family.

It didn't make Ava feel any better. Logan might not be sleeping with the beautiful and talented Kim but he was spending more time with her than his wife. Ava was beginning to get the sad feeling that perhaps he *preferred* it that way. Maybe…just maybe…Kim was more fun.

Ava decided then and there to remind her husband just how much fun she could be. She'd do it tonight.

CHAPTER NINETEEN

Tanner had left for home and the twins were put to bed. Peace and quiet reigned in a household that was usually loud and boisterous. It was a welcome respite at the end of the day.

Ava was still smarting from Logan's rejection earlier. He was a protective man so she wasn't in the least surprised that he'd said no to her helping, but she'd held onto a glimmer of hope. She wanted to be helpful with more than just dusty boxes of paper. She wanted to be a part of her husband's life. If he wouldn't come home and spend more time, then by God, she'd go to him.

She'd darn well refresh his memory about how enjoyable it was to spend time at home while she was at it. He'd become far too used to traveling, spending time with his *team*. That team got more of Logan's attention than she and the children did. Tonight she was going to do something about that.

Ava had taken a shower, shaved her legs and armpits, and rubbed a fragrant body lotion into her skin. She thought about the subtle approach but sometimes a woman simply had to say what she wanted and go for it. Besides, Logan was a straightforward man and he appreciated it when she didn't pussyfoot around a subject.

Pardon the pun.

Wrapping a towel around her naked body, she padded into the office where her absolutely gorgeous husband was poring over a stack of files. His blond hair had a few strands of gray now and there were more lines around his blue eyes but he was still the most spectacularly handsome man she'd ever known.

Time to quit, babe. I have plans.

He didn't turn around when she entered so she shut and locked the door behind her, a smile of pure glee on her face. This was going to be fun.

"Logan, can you look at something for me?"

"Uh sure, babe. Let me just mark where I left off. And by the way, you owe me a backrub, lasagna, and some chocolate mousse. The autopsy came back and the shooter was standing down the path." He turned just as she dropped her towel. It fell into a pool at her feet. Completely unimportant and unneeded. "What—"

His mouth fell open and then turned into a big, wolfish smile.

"I could look at you all day, babe. But I'd rather touch you. Get that gorgeous ass over here."

She couldn't think of one reason not to do just that.

"You sweet talker," she giggled, pressing herself against his fully clothed form and pulling his head down for a kiss. "How about a ride, cowboy? Fast and hard, just like you like it."

Ava liked it that way, too. His roughened hands slid down her body, sending the most erotic signals to her brain. Standing on tiptoe, her tongue snaked out to taste the salty tang of his skin as she pressed her lips to the hollow of his throat and breathed in his delicious scent.

If they could bottle that, every guy would get laid.

It felt incredibly naughty to be completely naked when he was fully dressed, but those clothes needed to come off. Her hands went to his waist and she popped open each button on his fly, rubbing her palm against his growing erection.

Logan groaned in anticipation when she fell to her knees and pulled him free from the denim and cotton boxers. He was long and thick in her hand, and the coil in her lower belly tightened as she traced a blue vein with her fingers. Bending her head, she followed that same path with her tongue while her fingers massaged the root. His balls had pulled up close to his body and if she kept up what she was doing he was going to explode soon.

Logan must have known that as well because she found herself lifted off her knees by two strong hands under her arms. He placed her on the desk, knocking the papers to the floor in his haste. Her ass hit the cool wood and it sent a shiver to her toes. She loved it when he was like this...as if they were the only two people left on this earth and he absolutely had to have her.

Shoving his jeans down slightly, Logan didn't waste any time. Positioning himself between her outspread thighs, he thrust in to the hilt with one stroke. They both cried out at the sensation, although it was muffled as their lips were locked together in a soul-searing kiss. His tongue imitated in her mouth what his cock was doing just a few feet below and she had to hold on for dear life, her fingers curling into his muscled shoulders.

He showed her no mercy, pounding into her as if she was sending him off to war and this might be the last time they were ever together. The veins in his neck were on display and his teeth were gritted together. He was trying to hold back so she could catch up.

The temperature in the room had soared and their skin was covered in a sheen of sweat. The only sounds were Logan's grunts, Ava's pants, and the vulgar slap of flesh on flesh. They were going at each other like animals, her fingernails scoring his back as she begged him to fuck her harder and faster. Anything. Just make her come.

The desk rattled on its legs and the lamp on the corner fell to the floor with a crash that neither of them even acknowledged. Logan nipped at that spot on her neck, sending a shot of electricity through her body and straight to her clit.

"Time to come, baby. You can do it. Come for me."

Her back arched and her head fell back, begging for more of his mouth. He gave it to her, his lips and teeth worrying at a rose-tipped nipple and that sent her off into space. She whirled around among the stars and clouds before eventually coming back to earth. At some point Logan had gone over as well, thrusting into her one last time and staying there. His chest was damp where she pressed her cheek as they crumpled from the desk to the floor in a tangle of arms and legs.

Eventually Logan stretched out on the cold hardwood and tucked Ava into his side. She stroked his stubbled jaw, content to just be here with him. They didn't need words to express what they both felt.

Their bodies cooled though, and the floor wasn't the most comfortable place for afterglow. Ava sat up and stretched her arms over her head, and then rubbed at her lower back.

"I think we might be getting too old for stuff like this."

"No way," Logan denied, sitting up but then groaning when his own back made a cracking noise. "Shit, maybe I am getting old."

Her palm cupped his jaw, turning his face toward her so she could look into his eyes.

"I can't wait to grow old with you."

Leaning down, he pressed his nose to hers. "And I can't wait to grow old with you either. We'll be two old wrinkled crime busters, sitting on the front porch in our rocking chairs and yelling at kids to get off our lawn."

It sounded like heaven as long as she was with him.

CHAPTER TWENTY

Ava helped Logan straighten his tie, brushing his hands away so she could do it herself. He was hopeless when it came to tying a Windsor knot. She wasn't in the greatest of moods but she was determined not to let it show.

Kim was here. Along with Tanner, of course.

Tonight was the night that Logan and Kim were going to the nightclub, pretending to be a couple. Ava would sit in the police car with Tanner listening in.

The whole idea was for the pretend couple to look prosperous, as if they had money to burn. Or in this case, gamble. Logan was dressed in his best suit and tie while Kim looked amazing in a tight red dress that clung to every curve. She'd definitely have plenty of male attention tonight, which was the plan. According to Natalie Denning, Cory had an eye for the ladies. Fancied himself something of a player. If Logan couldn't get him to talk, perhaps Kim could.

I could have done that, too.

Logan wasn't going to let her within a hundred feet of that club. He'd been clear on that. The only reason he was even going in himself was because Tanner was the sheriff in Springwood and the deputies were known as well. She'd reminded her husband that the deal was that he wouldn't be shot at any more. He'd assured her that he and Kim were simply going in to talk and get the lay of the land. They weren't going to be dragging anyone out of there to be questioned.

There was always a tiny chance that Logan would be recognized in the club and that could be dangerous, but it wasn't a big risk. The club was in Springwood and that was far enough that most residents of Corville wouldn't be driving there on a weeknight. Ava had a feeling its location had been one of the bonuses for Lyle. He wouldn't know anyone there and Mary would never find out.

"Say something," Tanner said, fiddling with the electronic equipment on the kitchen table. "Let's check the sound again now that you have your jacket on."

"Can you hear me, you old bastard?" Logan teased with a grin. "How's that?"

Tanner snorted and fiddled with a button. "Loud and clear. Damn, I love technology. It wasn't that long ago we would have had to shave your chest and tape wires to you. Now you just have to put a damn pen in your pocket."

Kim touched her ear. "Or wear an earring. These are genius. No one would ever guess that we're listening in."

"The internet is a wonderful place," Tanner laughed.

"And a little scary," Ava muttered. "Surveillance isn't even a skill anymore. Anyone can do it. It's kind of a letdown."

As the writer of mystery stories, it took the wind out of her sails a bit. The whole idea of surveillance in a book was the danger involved. With a pen and an earring there was no suspense. No buildup. No adrenaline rush.

"But much safer," Kim said with a smile. "I have to admit that I'm glad we don't have to be wired like in the movies."

"How do bad guys tell if they're being bugged?" Ava wondered out loud. "How do they know? I can hide a camera in a teddy bear and spy on the babysitter. No one is safe. Big Brother is always watching."

"I'm guessing that they don't say much in front of people they don't trust," Logan replied. "That's why I don't think we'll find out anything tonight. This is not so much information gathering as just seeing what we're dealing with. We need to know if Natalie is telling the truth. Lyle's attorney was no help."

After speaking with Lyle's lawyer, Logan had reported to the group that the divorce had been in flux. Lyle had at one point put the divorce on hold but then had called Marshall a few days before the shooting and said he wanted to meet. Was he going to change his mind and go ahead with the divorce? They'd never know.

"Did you find anything in the financials?" Tanner asked. "Anything that pointed to a gambling habit?"

Ava had been through those documents until she was cross-eyed. "Not that I've found. But of course, that assumes that I have all the information. We have what we've subpoenaed. It's the old conundrum of we don't know what we don't know. Some things we know we don't know, but this? We're flying blind here."

Logan checked his tie one last time in the mirror. "I've got Jared doing some digging. If Lyle had any hidden accounts of money, he'll find it."

Tanner's lips twisted and he rubbed his chin. "I hate to ask this, but do you think your sister knew about the gambling, Ava?"

Sighing, she plopped down into a chair at the table. "It's nothing I haven't asked myself since we heard Natalie's story. But I don't think she did...or does, I guess I should say. Mary has something of a temper and I think if she found out that Lyle had lost a bunch of money and owed dangerous people she would have been screaming from the rooftops. We'd still be hearing her bitch about that."

Kim's brow rose. "According to witnesses, she did chase her own husband out of the house with a gun."

Mary was still a suspect, although Ava wasn't happy about it.

"True, and that doesn't help the way she's perceived by the police. But the one thing Mary loves more than anything is to be the victim in a scenario. If Lyle had done this, you'd think she'd tell everyone. My mom, my dad. The local butcher. Hiding in the bushes and shooting her husband just doesn't fit with her personality."

"In other words, she'd go after you head on," Logan added. "She wouldn't hide like a criminal. She'd think what she was doing was justified."

Almost like Wade. Ava wasn't blind to her sister's faults but even she didn't want to think that her sister was a sociopath with narcissistic tendencies.

Tanner tucked the receiver under his arm and stood. "Are we ready to go?"

Logan smiled and stood right next to Kim. "I think so. How do we look? Like a believable couple?"

Sadly, yes. They made a beautiful pair.

Ava didn't like it one bit.

CHAPTER TWENTY-ONE

Logan wasn't the most self-aware man. He spent far too much time with his nose in case files to often take a look at the world around him. His wife's moods were a mystery a great deal of the time as well. Ava could be the sweetest thing ever and the next minute mean and surly as a snake, especially when she was sleep deprived from working on a book deadline.

But even he could tell that Ava wasn't the happiest of campers. He knew why, of course. She'd wanted to accompany him into the club but he wasn't going to allow that. Far too dangerous. He shouldn't be doing it either but there wasn't anyone else. Sure, Jason could have sent another agent along with Kim but this was easier. Besides, this would hopefully be his last case with Kim. She'd be getting her full-fledged status soon and Logan would be taking the new position.

The room was smoky and loud, a combination that grated on Logan's nerves. There was a time in his life that he would have enjoyed this but those days were long gone. He liked the peace and quiet of an evening at home now. As much quiet as a man could get anyway with twins tearing up the house.

"Looks like a happening place," Kim remarked as he led her

toward a table that had an excellent view of the large room. The club was busy for a weeknight but not packed and they were able to slip into seats without any trouble. A pretty waitress took their drink order and then melted away somewhere in the direction of the bar, which took up an entire wall at the front. "I don't see him. Do you?"

Luckily Natalie had shown him a photo of Cory on her phone so Logan knew what the man looked like. What he didn't know was whether anything the young woman said was the truth. According to her, there was a gambling den upstairs. From their vantage point, he should be able to see if anyone came or went from the second floor.

Leaning close to Kim as if he was whispering in her ear, he spoke just loud enough that he hoped Tanner could hear him in the car across the street. "We're inside and so far I haven't seen anyone go upstairs, nor have we seen Cory."

The waitress came back with their drinks – beer for Logan and a martini for Kim. Since they were playing the part of people with more money than sense, he tipped the young girl far too generously and then gave her a broad wink. The waitress gave him a sultry smile in return and tucked the bill into her bra. Her hips swayed as she walked away and she shot him another glance over her shoulder. Just as she disappeared behind the bar, he watched as another waitress climbed the stairs carrying a full tray of drinks.

"Look," Logan said, smiling at Kim but his gaze was on the far side of the room. "That's a hell of a lot of drinks to be taking upstairs."

Before Kim could reply, a man came down the stairs and headed toward the exit.

"Looks like Natalie might have been telling the truth," Kim replied.

"But was she telling the truth about everything? We just don't know yet. I really want to find a way to get up there but I doubt that's going to be possible our first time here."

"You may have to have someone vouch for you. That's what I'd do if I had an illegal gambling club."

"Invitation only," Logan agreed, almost gleeful to see a couple climbing the stairs. Something was definitely going on. "What if we just went up there? What do you think they'd do?"

"Throw our asses out. If we're lucky."

Ava was listening in to this conversation and she wouldn't be happy to hear him talking about taking stupid risks. It was just that he hated being in Corville and the sooner he solved Lyle's murder, the sooner he could get the hell out of town and back home. Didn't she feel it too? The animosity? The resentment? People hated him and tolerated Ava. He'd upended their comfortable little world and they weren't likely to forgive him whether he found Lyle's murderer or not.

"So we won't do that. Any ideas?"

This was Kim's final exam, after all. He should be letting her take the lead but in a situation like this it simply didn't come naturally to him.

"I could go powder my nose. Maybe you can get one of the waitresses or customers to talk."

As ideas went it wasn't too bad. Kim slipped out of her chair and headed of the ladies room, leaving Logan at the table. He eyed their young and pretty waitress from afar, letting her feel the weight of his stare. When she noticed, she turned and gave him a wink. It was almost too easy. Sitting back down, he sipped at his rapidly warming beer. The drink was really only for show, not for relaxation.

The girl sidled up next to him when she was done with the other table. "I think you could do better."

"Do you? I think so, too."

The young woman slid a cold beer he hadn't ordered in front of him. "She doesn't seem to appreciate you."

Logan gave her a mocking smile. "Maybe I'm a total asshole."

The waitress ran her fingers down between her cleavage where she'd tucked that fifty.

"I doubt it. I bet you're just...misunderstood."

"That's exactly what I am." He leaned back, pretending to get a better look at her. "What's your name, pretty girl?"

Ava had to be about to blow a gasket right about now listening to this. I'll make it up to her.

"Cindy." The girl propped her hand on the table so that her breasts were almost falling out of her tight white blouse. "What's yours?"

"Logan," he replied, taking a swig of the fresh beer. "Thanks for the beer, baby. What do I owe you?"

"That one's on the house."

That wouldn't do. He was supposed to be throwing around cash. Reaching into his pocket, he pulled out another fifty. "Then this is just for you, gorgeous."

Her cheeks turned pink either from the compliment or plain greed. Cindy tucked it away with the other one but kept her hand there, stroking the top of her breast.

"I get off at two."

That was straight to the point. No foreplay, baby?

"Going home to your husband?" His gaze fell on her bare left hand. "Or a boyfriend?"

"I'm free as a bird." She leaned farther toward him, her lips next to his ear. Ava would probably still be able to hear her. "And ready to party."

He checked his watch, an inexpensive Rolex knockoff but he

hoped Cindy couldn't tell the difference. "I'll have to ditch my girl at some point but that's easy. She doesn't like to stay out much past midnight. I can send her home in a cab. It's only eleven now. I could kill some time upstairs."

If Cindy was surprised that he knew about the gambling room she didn't act it. If anything, she behaved as if this was a common request. Perhaps it was.

"If you want into the poker game, there's a minimum."

He didn't ask what it was. It didn't matter.

"That's fine. Can you get me in, darlin'?"

"Sure, follow me."

This was turning out to be a productive evening after all.

Tanner clapped his hands together with glee. "He's going to get in there. I never dreamed he'd get in the first night. Looks like throwing around some cash was the key."

Money talked, that was for sure, and Logan looked every inch the prosperous businessman. Not that it mattered. Women flirted with Ava's husband on a regular basis even when she was standing right next to him. She'd grown used to it and in fact, it amused her. Logan, on the other hand, usually didn't even notice. If he did, he didn't care. Clearly he'd been paying attention this evening to little Cindy.

"How's he going to get Kim in with him?" Ava asked. "He can't leave her alone."

Impatiently she waited, listening to the background noise of the nightclub almost drown out their small talk. She caught something about needing another drink but the rest was either too low or too garbled to make out.

Ava leaned down, straining to hear. Cindy and Logan were speaking but she couldn't decipher what they were saying.

Stupid technology.

All it took was a massive sound system playing songs from the eighties with way too much bass and she couldn't hear a thing.

"What are they saying?"

Tanner too was leaning in close, his brows pinched together in concentration. "I can't tell. They're talking and it doesn't sound angry or anything."

They could be discussing the weather or Cindy could be trying to make plans for after closing time.

Sorry, hon. Logan's busy.

"You're going upstairs?"

Kim's voice came through loud and clear.

"No, we're going upstairs." Logan must have moved his jacket out of the way and now the pen was easily picking up the conversation. "You're not staying down here alone."

"It sounds boring."

Kim sounded convincing as the pissed off girlfriend who didn't want to follow her man anywhere. As much as Ava wished it was herself with Logan, she couldn't deny that she felt confident with the other woman by his side.

"Just try it for a little while. If you don't like it, I'll call you a cab or an Uber."

"Fine."

More noise and the sound of footsteps. Muffled voices from a distance. There was the deep voice of a man and then the beat of the music faded. A more subdued noise palette took its place. The soft murmur of conversation and the tinkling of laughter in the distance.

Logan was in. A shot of adrenaline ran up her spine. He might be able to speak to someone who had seen Lyle there, or even better he might get Cory to talk.

She heard him order a drink for both of them and then Kim said they should walk around. Mingle. Lose some money.

"Sounds like a good idea. Best place to lose money fast is probably the roulette– Wait...we need to abort the mission. Did you hear me, Tanner? Abort. Right now. Kim and I are out of here."

Logan must have been recognized. Damn it.

Now he had to get out of there alive.

CHAPTER TWENTY-TWO

Logan wasn't his father-in-law's favorite person and that was fine. He'd grown used to Bruce's bitching and complaining about every little thing. He didn't like Logan's profession. He didn't like Logan's motorcycle. He didn't like it when Logan had married Ava. He sure as hell didn't like it when they'd moved out of Corville and ended up just outside of Seattle. Since Bruce had retired a few years ago he had only become worse, basically unhappy about everyone and everything. Poor Carol was a wonderful woman and she deserved far better.

So it was a complete and utter shock when Logan had surveyed the gamblers in the secret room and found his holier-than-thou church deacon father-in-law playing poker. It was – literally – the last thing he'd expected. If a purple gorilla had been dealing blackjack, Logan would have been less surprised.

Not knowing how Bruce would react, Logan had no choice but to pull the plug on the operation. His father-in-law wasn't exactly known for his mild manners and discretion, although he'd been keeping a mighty big secret lately. He doubted that this was Bruce's first time here. He looked far too comfortable.

Luckily Kim didn't ask too many questions, quickly catching

on that something was amiss. She immediately feigned stomach cramps and Logan hustled her down the stairs and out of the front doors before Cindy could do more than make a few half-hearted protests. He bundled Kim into the car and hightailed it out of the parking lot trying to think of a good way to break the news to his wife.

Hey honey, your dad has a gambling problem. Oh, and by the way, he probably knew about Lyle and his gambling habit. His girlfriend, too.

This was going to make Thanksgiving awkward as fuck.

He pulled into the parking lot right next to Tanner's SUV. They'd chosen a rendezvous spot ahead of time.

Tanner and Ava jumped out of the truck the moment they pulled alongside his vehicle.

"What happened?" Ava's gaze swept him up and down. "Are you okay? Did someone recognize you?"

Scraping his fingers through his hair, Logan blew out a long breath. He owed them an explanation but dammit, this wasn't going to go well.

"I'll explain if you give me a minute."

All three of them were looking at him expectantly. Kim had been patient so far but he couldn't expect that to continue for much longer.

"First of all, great thinking, Kim," he praised. "We got out of there smoothly. I appreciate your help."

"No problem. Glad that we got out of there without any questions."

He leaned a hip against the hood of his car. "I did see someone I knew in there and I didn't know how they would react to seeing me, so I pulled the plug on our operation."

Tanner nodded grimly. "We'll just call Griffin or Reed. They might be able to lend us some men that wouldn't be known there."

"Unfortunately, that's not our only problem now."

Ava frowned. "Do you think Cory suspected something?"

"Not in the least. No, this…this is…personal, baby. Maybe you and I should go someplace and talk about it."

Her sharp gaze ran from Tanner to Kim and then to Logan.

"Personal? Do you mean that I know who was there?"

Logan nodded, already pissed off at Bruce Hayworth putting him in this position. Ava was going to be upset. Mary was going to be upset. Carol was going to be upset.

That was a whole lot of upset that one man had caused with his thoughtlessness.

"You might as well just tell me because they're going to find out eventually. There aren't any secrets in a murder investigation, remember? That's what we told Mary."

Yep, Logan was going to kick Bruce's ass.

"It was your dad."

Ava's eyes widened and then her lips flattened into a straight line.

"My father? He was there?"

"He was at the poker table. I don't think he saw me but I definitely saw him."

No one said anything for the longest time. Ava appeared to be grappling with what she'd learned about her own parent and Kim and Tanner were respectfully giving her the space to do that.

"You did the right thing," Ava finally replied. "I doubt he would have reacted well to seeing you there. With Kim especially. He wouldn't have understood that you were on an assignment."

Shit, it hadn't even occurred to Logan that Bruce would think he was cheating with Kim. He'd been worried about the gambling angle.

Tanner cleared his throat loudly. "What do you want to do now?"

Have a drink. Maybe two.

"We need to speak with Bruce, obviously. He must have known about Lyle's gambling habit."

"And probably Natalie as well," Ava said, her tone hard. "I never realized my father was this skilled at secret keeping. He's just full of surprises."

"Let's hope there aren't any more, babe."

"What about Cory?" Kim asked, nodding back toward the nightclub. "We'll still need to talk to him. He's a possible suspect."

"I can answer that," Tanner said. "I now have probable cause to drag his sorry ass in for questioning. I'm going to get that back room shut down as quickly as possible. With the possibility of federal charges hanging over his head maybe Cory will talk."

But first Logan needed to speak with Bruce, and there was no way he was going to be able to keep Ava from not attending that discussion. This was going to get ugly.

The reason for Ava's sleepless night was sitting at his kitchen table and lying through his teeth. If she'd done the same thing when she was a kid, he would have washed her mouth out with soap and sent her to her room without supper.

"I didn't know about Lyle's gambling," Bruce protested, his face almost purple. "And I absolutely didn't know about any other women. I don't think Lyle would do that."

Ava rolled her eyes at Logan before turning back to her father.

"Right, because he was such a fine, upstanding citizen. Did

you know he wanted Logan to look the other way when he realized that Wade was the vigilante killer?"

Bruce had the good sense to look down at the floor but Ava wasn't done with him. She had a lifetime of his lectures saved up, constantly telling her right from wrong, and she wasn't going to let this go easily.

"Dad, look me in the eye and tell me you didn't know that Lyle was cheating and gambling. Can you do it? You can't, can you?"

"Bruce," Logan said, keeping his tone as nonjudgmental as possible. "We need to find Lyle's killer and you might know something that would help us."

Bruce's head snapped up. "That was my first time there."

It was amazing how easily her father lied. It made Ava wonder how much practice he'd had over the years.

"We're going to bring in the manager of the nightclub. If we ask him about you will he say it was your first time there?"

The air seemed to leak out of Bruce, his shoulders slumping in defeat. "No."

Flipping a chair around, Logan straddled it so he was facing Bruce. "Now we're getting somewhere. We need the truth. I won't settle for anything less and neither will your daughter. Not to mention Mary and Carol."

Bruce shook his head and Ava was startled by how Bruce had aged ten years in mere minutes. His previously red cheeks were now ashen and his eyes bloodshot. He looked old and sad and not in the least intimidating.

"I didn't do anything all that bad."

Bruce's voice was barely a whisper.

"That's good. Real good. Now let's start at the beginning. Did Lyle take you to the gambling house the first time or did you take him?"

Her father's throat bobbed as he swallowed hard. "He took me. About a year ago. I was always complaining about how bored I was. He said that he knew something that was more exciting than puttering around in the garage."

Lyle had taken her father. But Bruce still had to have known about Natalie.

"Do you know how long Lyle had been going before he took you?" Logan asked.

Bruce shook his head sadly. "I don't know. It was awhile, though. Everyone knew him there. They all greeted him by his first name."

Rubbing his chin, Logan nodded. "Okay, this is good information. Did you know that Lyle owed a lot of money?"

"Yes." Bruce's voice was barely audible. "I was trying to help him."

"Oh, Dad. What did you do?"

Ava couldn't see how her father could help Lyle unless he was willing to give him a whole heck of a lot of cash, which Bruce Hayworth didn't have. Had he been playing cards to win back the money?

"How? How could you help Lyle raise that kind of cash?" Ava queried. Her parents weren't wealthy but perhaps he'd dipped into their retirement savings.

"I'm a decent card player."

Logan's gaze flickered over to Ava, his eyes sad. "That's why Lyle asked you to go with him, isn't it? He wanted help winning back the money."

"Not at first." Bruce shook his head in denial. "But then later... When the debts really began to pile up and they were threatening him, although not so much in the last several months."

Ave pounced on that. "With death?"

Bruce frowned. "I don't think so. They said they'd rough him up and he'd be hurt bad. They threatened to tell Mary. They wanted him to sell some of the Bryson assets."

"Why didn't he?" Logan shot back. "That would have been the sensible move."

"There wasn't anything left to sell, really. I think he must have sold a few things to keep them at bay because they've left him alone for awhile."

Such a simple statement but it was sad, too. At one time the Bryson family had ruled this little town like local royalty.

"What about Natalie?" Logan asked. "You did know about her, right? You had to know."

Bruce nodded slowly as if admitting it was painful. It should be.

"I knew. He and Mary were always fighting and yelling at one another. He wanted to have kids and she didn't."

Was her father actually defending Lyle? Jesus, Ava could hardly stand this conversation.

"Was he going to divorce Mary?" she demanded. "She thinks they were reconciling but that's not what Natalie thinks. What's the truth?"

"He didn't know what to do. He wanted to be free, but he hated the idea of going through the divorce and I was trying to talk him out of it."

So that still gave both Mary and Natalie a motive. Lyle wouldn't make up his mind.

Logan stood and pushed the chair back into place at the table. "We're going to need more details, but before we go any further I need to know what you were doing the morning Lyle was shot."

Bruce's eyes went round and his mouth fell open. "You think I did it? I need an alibi?"

"I think you do," Logan stated flatly.

Bruce wasn't taking the news well. His once gray skin had turned a ruddy shade and his breathing was loud and agitated. "You think I would shoot my own son-in-law?"

To her husband's credit he didn't crack a smile, simply staying expressionless. If her father had ever caught Logan doing some of the things they used to do before they were legally wed, she had no doubt Bruce would have met him at the door with a shotgun.

"I think that Lyle cheating on your oldest daughter might be considered a motive by some. It's in your best interests for us to clear you as soon as possible."

"I was trying to help him," Bruce protested. "I wouldn't shoot him."

"Then where were you that morning?" Logan pressed. "Can anybody vouch for your whereabouts?"

"I wasn't home. I was at the Rotary Club Breakfast. There should be dozens of witnesses. The speaker was the local high school's class valedictorian. He gave a speech on service to the community."

Ava knew a moment of complete and total gratitude. She didn't have to worry about her father being a killer. Small mercies and all of that.

"Are we done here?" Bruce asked. "I think I've had about enough of this and you."

He didn't seem to understand the seriousness of what was going on.

"Dad, we've only just got started. We have lots more questions."

CHAPTER TWENTY-THREE

Logan and Ava left her father's home, picked up the kids, and then headed straight for Mary and Lyle's house. Mary had to be told the news and neither of them was looking forward to that conversation.

"Do you think he has a girlfriend, too?"

Logan looked over at his wife sitting in the passenger seat of the car. Despite all she'd been hit with in the past twenty-four hours she'd been admirably calm. Almost too calm.

"I think this isn't a subject we should be having with the kids in the backseat."

Ava looked over her shoulder and sighed. "They're watching Scooby Doo. I doubt they're even paying attention."

"It was your idea to get them a tablet. I didn't have a tablet when I was six. I had a bat and ball."

And I walked to school uphill in the snow. Both ways.

"Times have changed. Kids play differently. And they do have a bat and ball. They play outside quite a bit, but in the car and on airplanes they can't play baseball."

She made sense but he didn't have to like it. He wanted his kids to understand and embrace technology but it was disturbing that they seemed to love it so much. Way more than they should.

Logan glanced over his shoulder at his two children, their heads close together as they giggled at the antics of the talking cartoon dog who solved crimes. If only it was as easy as *setting a trap* and letting it all go awry.

"I don't think he has a girlfriend."

Logan kept his voice low, although Ava was surely correct in that the twins weren't listening.

"For Mom's sake, I hope not, especially when they were trying to work things out not long ago. But he did know all about Lyle and never said anything. I'm not sure I can forgive him for that."

He'd thought about the situation and had come to a conclusion. "I know you're angry and upset, babe, but...he's your dad. And he's not young anymore. I don't want to see you do something drastic and then wish you hadn't later."

Like if Bruce suddenly died. Ava would never forgive herself if he passed away while they weren't speaking to one another.

"Since when do you take Dad's side?"

It was kind of funny. Logan and Bruce didn't agree on the color of the sky, yet here he was kinda sorta defending his father-in-law. Bruce had done wrong and Logan wouldn't give him a pass on that, but he didn't want to see Ava make a knee-jerk decision that she'd regret later.

"I'm taking your side. I'm thinking about you, not Bruce. Frankly, he has to deal with the consequences of his poor decisions. But taking your love away from him probably isn't the answer. He knows you don't approve."

"He's a hypocrite."

The words were said under Ava's breath but he still heard them.

"Yes, and from the look on his face when we questioned

him he knows that. I don't think you'll be getting any lectures from him any time soon, so there's that."

"It's so out of character for him," she sighed, reaching across the seat and placing her hand on his. He immediately wound their fingers together. Her skin felt warm and reassuring, just as it always did. Ava brought peace to his sometimes crazy world. He only hoped he could do that for her today.

"He was bored. He just wasn't thinking. He wanted some excitement."

"He got it," Ava snorted. "He thought he was James Bond, frequenting an illegal gambling den. My poor mother."

Carol was the real victim in all of this. She'd put up with more than any woman should through the years. They'd been talking divorce for a long time but it looked inevitable now. Logan didn't think Ava would forgive him if she found out he was lying behind her back. In fact, she'd kick his ass from here to Puget Sound and back again.

"What are you going to say to Mary?"

They'd already decided that Ava would be the one to tell her sister while Logan kept the twins busy in the backyard. Mary was incredibly unpredictable. She might blow up or she might shrug and move on. But he did need to ask her about that insurance policy. She'd never mentioned it in all of their conversations about Lyle's death.

"She already knows about Natalie, so no surprise there. I'm not going to tell her that maybe Lyle was going to go ahead with the divorce. It won't help and we really don't know for sure. I will tell her about the gambling debts. She deserves to know. If she hasn't exploded at that point, I'll tell her about Dad."

"Sounds like a decent plan. I need to talk to her about the insurance policy."

"I'll do that," Ava assured him. "It's going to come up when

I talk about the money issues. I need to know if she was aware just how bad their financial situation was."

That everything worth selling was basically gone. At least according to Bruce via Lyle.

But Logan had been lied to before by the Bryson family. He wouldn't put it past them to hide their assets so no one could get to them.

"Let me know if you need my help." Logan pulled up into Mary's driveway. "You don't have to do this, you know. I can do it."

Ava had already been through quite a lot and it wasn't even lunchtime yet.

"No, I'll do it. I need to be the one."

What a lousy fucking day. This was why he didn't want to come back to Corville. The only good thing that had ever happened here was meeting Ava.

Ava closely watched Mary's expression, waiting for anger or tears or some other strong emotion but saw none. It was as if Ava had announced to her sister that she didn't like ketchup. Mild surprise but no real reaction either way. Ava didn't know whether to be relieved or alarmed.

"I knew Lyle was up to more than just another woman," Mary finally said, staring out of the back window of the living room that looked over the yard where Logan played with twins. "I just didn't know what it was. Do you know how much he lost?"

"Not yet. We're going to bring in the club owner and question him."

"Will they come after me for the money?"

Ava hadn't expected that question.

"No! I don't think so. Logan didn't say anything about that."
She couldn't help her curiosity though. "Are you planning to stay
in Corville?"

"This is where the family business is. This is where Mom and
Dad live."

"With the insurance money you could go anywhere, do anything. You could start over."

There. She'd dropped the bomb right in the middle of Mary's
flowered furniture. Time to see what her sister would say.

"I suppose I could but it was intended to keep the business
running."

"Half a million is a lot of money."

Mary shrugged and returned to her seat on the overstuffed
couch. "Aaron has the same policy. They took them out at the
same time."

"But you're the beneficiary, not the company. Or Aaron."

"So? I was his wife."

Ava sighed and pushed her hair off of her face. Mary didn't
seem to get it. "It adds to your motive. This doesn't help us clear
your name."

The anger that Ava had been expecting earlier finally made
an appearance. Mary's face turned red and her lips pressed
together tightly. "I didn't kill my husband for the money."

"Or because he was cheating. Or gambling. Do you see
where I'm going here? You had plenty of motive, Mary. We need
to find a way to clear your name but you've got to help us here."

"I loved my husband," Mary declared, sitting ramrod
straight, her entire body stiff. "I don't believe that he was going
to ask for a divorce either. We were really happy the last few
months."

Ava hated to be the bad guy but she had no choice. "I told
you that he was still in touch with Natalie right up until the day

he was shot."

"That doesn't mean they were sleeping together. Maybe she was helping him with the gambling debt."

Denial wasn't just a river in Egypt. It ran right through Corville as well. Ava dropped the subject and picked up another grenade, lobbing it between them.

"What about Daddy?"

Looking away, Mary took her time answering. "While I'm upset about that, I'll find a way to get over it. We're family. If Lyle taught me anything in the years that we were together it's that family is the most important thing."

"Everything we've found so far doesn't help you in the least. It looks worse than ever for you. Is there anything you can tell me that might help? Something you may have forgotten? Anything at all? It could even be the smallest thing. You're in deep trouble here, sis. All the signs point to you."

As it was, Logan was going to have to talk Drake out of arresting Mary but she would probably be brought in for official questioning.

"No, there's nothing I haven't told you."

"Then I suggest you get a lawyer. A good one."

Mary had the audacity to smile at moment like this. "I'm not worried. I'm innocent. You and Logan will eventually prove it. Besides, no jury in Corville would convict me. They all know what kind of person I am."

Ava wished she had her sister's confidence.

CHAPTER TWENTY-FOUR

C olt had finished brushing his teeth and was getting tucked
up into bed by Ava while Logan supervised Ella's dental
hygiene. Dressed in pink shortie pajamas that just perfectly
matched her toothbrush his daughter swished and spit into the
sink. He placed her toothbrush into the holder and helped her
wipe down her face, noticing that she'd picked up a few freckles
this summer. Ava was a stickler for sunscreen but freckles always
found a way. He'd had them when he was about her age, too.

"Did you catch the killer yet, Daddy?"

What in the—?

"I'm not sure what you mean, jellybean."

His pretty little girl rolled her eyes at him. *Rolled her eyes.* He
had some fun to look forward to when she was a teenager. Six
years old and she already thought he was an idiot.

"Daddy, I know why we're here. You never want to come to
see Grandma and Grandpa. I heard you tell Mommy. You're
going to find the bad guy like you always do."

At least she thought he was good at his job. But it did bring
up the question of just how much his children knew about what
he did for a living. He and Ava didn't discuss the details very

often around them. He could only imagine how they perceived his career. He was gone for long stretches and while Ava's job was much more sedate she was as deeply entrenched in the criminal world as he was. She did copious amounts of research for every story and it would have been a shock if the twins hadn't picked up on that despite their efforts to keep them away from the *family business*.

He was surprised, however, that they were aware he didn't want to come to Corville. They were growing up fast and they had Ava's brains. Smart as a whip, they understood far more than he'd given them credit for. They joked that the twins were six going on sixteen but he was beginning to think that it was nothing to laugh at.

"I'm going to try and catch the bad guy."

He'd keep his answers in simple terms a child could understand but already he could see intelligence in his daughter's eyes that was far beyond her chronological age. She saw things that other children ignored or didn't care about. Brianna seemed to notice all the little details of a situation and she'd managed to put the puzzle together quite well. Something her mother excelled at.

"You'll get him," Brianna pronounced confidently. "Mommy says you're amazing at catching bad guys."

Mommy said that? His chest puffed up with pride. She wasn't so bad herself.

"When did you hear Mommy say that?"

"When she was talking to Aunt Kaylee on the phone."

Thank God that's all they'd been talking about. Kaylee's books were rather…steamy…and she sometimes asked Ava for advice when it came to a scene. Logan had a feeling that some of his sex life had made it into a few books but frankly he'd been afraid to find out for sure.

Sitting down on the closed toilet, Logan smoothed down

Brianna's hair. Like her mother's, it had a tendency to curl in the heat and humidity.

"Did Mommy know that you were listening to her conversation?"

Wrinkling her nose, Brianna shook her head. Jesus, she looked so much like Ava.

"I was supposed to be in bed sleeping, but I wanted a drink of water."

Brianna always wanted a drink of water. Sleeping was the enemy to her.

"Where was I?"

His daughter shrugged. "At work. Like always. Are you going to read us a story tonight?"

At work. Like always.

He was planning to do something about that. No more being away for days or even weeks at a time. He was missing too much. He was missing Ava. Did she miss him? Or had she become used to his absences? Did she prefer him to be gone?

"It's rude to listen in to other people's conversations, sweet pea. Don't do that. And yes, I'm going to read you a story. What do you want to hear?"

"The story about the princess." Again. He knew it by heart. Along with the one about the naughty dinosaurs and the one about the rabbit that wouldn't eat his vegetables. He swung Brianna up onto his back and headed to the bedroom. "Daddy, have you ever shot anyone?"

Abruptly stopping in the hallway, he stared up at his innocent little angel. Jesus, where had that question come from? What in the hell did she think he did for a living? Why was she even thinking about this stuff?

"Brianna–" He broke off, not even sure how to respond. He had indeed shot and killed people. First when he was in the military and then as a cop, but he wasn't sure that this was information his six-year-old needed in her life. "You shouldn't ask someone that question."

His daughter wasn't going to be deterred, however. "Colt and I watched a show on television and the sheriff shot several bad guys."

That's it. No more television. Ever, or at least until she was about thirty. He was always telling Ava that the kids watched too much even though she already controlled their screen time like a military drill sergeant. Apparently even a few hours a day was far too much.

"What were you watching? You shouldn't watch that anymore."

"*Bonanza*," she replied immediately. "You said that show was okay."

Christ on a cracker, he'd thought it was. He'd urged the kids to watch older show reruns thinking they'd be more innocent. Maybe Ava was right to let them watch *Spongebob*. No one was ever shot in the street standing next to a house made out of a pineapple.

"I think you should read more. Television will rot your brain."

Hadn't his mother said the very same thing to him when he'd sat in front of the television set every Saturday watching hour after hour of mind-numbing entertainment? Hell, he'd watched *Bonanza* and look how he'd turned out. He was doing fine.

He'd also watched television with Wade and look how *he'd* turned out. Maybe television didn't matter after all.

Brianna giggled and patted him on the head. "Ewww, rotting brains. That's icky."

Kids loved farts and gore.

Ava popped her head out of Colt's bedroom. "Are you ready for your night-night story?"

Logan placed Brianna on the floor and she ran to the end of Colt's bed and curled up, waiting for another retelling of the princess adventures.

"What took you so long?" Ava asked, reaching for a few books off the shelf. "Did she give you a hard time about brushing her teeth? She's usually really good about that."

Logan shook his head, deliberately keeping his voice down. "She brushed without complaint. No, she asked me if I'd caught the shooter yet. Then she asked me if I'd ever shot anyone because she saw an episode of *Bonanza* where the sheriff killed the bad guys."

"I told you those old westerns were violent," Ava sighed. "They've both had a lot of questions lately about your job and what I write. I think Colt read a part of one of my chapters that I was working on a few weeks ago although I doubt he understood it. How did you answer?"

Suddenly Logan wished his children hadn't learned to read so early or were so good at it.

"I told her not to watch *Bonanza* anymore and that she shouldn't ask people those type of questions."

Ava gave him a dubious look. "And she bought that? I'm all for them not watching old westerns anymore but it's only natural for them to have curiosity about what we do, Logan. One of their friend's parents is a doctor, another is a pastry chef. We're ass deep in crime. They were going to figure it out sooner or later."

Later was better.

"She asked me if I've killed anyone. Why couldn't she ask where babies come from or the meaning of life?" He took a sharp breath. "And they know I don't want to be here."

"We've never talked down to them. When they've asked us questions about babies or life or why the sky is blue, we've always tried to tell them the truth in an age appropriate way. Maybe it's time they heard a new story."

She wasn't saying…

"The one about how mommy and daddy met." He opened his mouth to object but she held up her hand. "Hear me out. We won't give them all the dirty details that will give them nightmares and keep them from sleeping for the next five or ten years. But they're asking for information about their parents. Isn't there a way we can give it to them without scarring them for life? There has to be."

His gaze moved from his wife to his children, whispering and giggling as Colt showed Brianna something he'd drawn. They were so young…so innocent. His heart squeezed in his chest at the thought of life coming along and ruining all of that. Keeping them safe was his first and most important responsibility. He wanted them to stay young forever but that's not how this worked. His job – and Ava's – was to prepare them to leave. That was the funny thing about parenthood. It was his job to raise his children to grow up and not need him anymore. It didn't matter if he needed them.

They were only six. Couldn't they stay happy and naive for just a little while longer? Better yet, a lot longer. The world turned entirely too fast and he couldn't stop it no matter how much he wanted to. But he could slow it down just a little bit.

"They're too young," Logan finally replied. "They know all they need to know for now. It will just scare them."

It didn't matter anyway. In a few weeks or months, he'd be off of the road and home every night. Just another paper pusher in an office, or in his case a computer geek, digging up details and history.

Better that they think of their father as boring as hell rather than some outlaw chasing, white-hat wearing lawman. He didn't want them to think he was any sort of hero because he wasn't. He didn't want them to emulate him when choosing their careers. His children were going to grow up and have regular jobs like normal people. Chasing criminals and solving mysteries were out of the question.

CHAPTER TWENTY-FIVE

Just like so many years before, Ava was in the sheriff's office watching the questioning on a live television feed and Logan was in the conference room talking to Cory Eldridge.

"I really liked Lyle. He was a good guy," Cory said, nodding for emphasis. "He first came in just to hang out with Nat but then we got to talking. He was funny and he even did some work on the roof as a favor. No way would I have had him killed. I considered him a friend."

Logan carefully controlled his expression. He didn't want to give anything away, positive or negative. He was just glad this guy was talking.

"Your friend owed you a lot of money."

Cory's lips twisted. "He did and my partners were starting to get antsy about that. Lyle had a bad run during basketball season and the football playoffs. Normally he was pretty good at picking winners but he had a nasty run of luck in the winter and spring. I know he would have turned it around, though."

"So you kept giving him credit?"

"He was good for it."

Cory believed that. Did the whole town? Were the Brysons

deliberately creating the illusion that they were still a family dynasty or did they actually have the money but tied up in the business? Lyle didn't have it personally, that was for sure. Logan and Ava had been through their finances with a fine-toothed comb. The business made money but wasn't awash in cash.

"Is that what he told you?"

"He said that he was going to get it for us but that he had to do it without letting his brother know."

"And you believed him?"

Cory shifted restlessly in his chair. "Yeah, I believed him. The family has money. He'd come through before so I had no reason to believe he wouldn't again."

Before?

"He'd owed you in the past?"

Chuckling, Cory grinned widely. "That's how this works. You make bets and you pay if you lose. Sure, we give people some latitude but eventually you hit your credit limit. We're not American Express here."

He was almost afraid to ask but he had to. "What was Lyle's credit limit?"

More shifting in his chair. Cory didn't want to answer. Tough.

"It...depended. I mean...at the beginning it was much lower."

Logan leaned forward in his chair, his hands resting on the cool wood of the table between himself and Cory. "How much did Lyle owe?"

It looked like it was painful for Cory to answer. "About a hundred thousand, give or take."

"A hundred thousand?" Logan asked, clarifying the other man's statement. "Lyle owed you and your partners a hundred thousand dollars? That's a hell of a lot more than a few bad bets.

That's a shitload of bad luck right there."

What had Lyle been thinking?

Cory sat up straight, his hands coming up in front of him in a sort of defensive posture.

"We weren't worried. We knew he'd take care of it. We don't kill people when they owe us money. That's bad business."

"You just break a few legs."

"I have never broken anyone's legs."

It was Logan's turn to smile. "I don't doubt that. You probably have someone else do your dirty work."

"I liked Lyle Bryson," Eldridge said again, his tone firm. "He'd always paid in the past and he would have paid us this time. We're the ones that are out the money now. With him dead we have to write off the debt. Besides, I have an alibi."

They always did.

"I bet you do. An airtight one. Care to share?"

A sly smile bloomed on the other man's face. "I was in bed with a lovely lady. Busy, if you know what I mean."

I do know what you mean and it makes me nauseous.

Ripping a piece of paper off of a spiral notebook, Logan pushed it and a pencil across to Eldridge. "We'll need her name and number to confirm."

"You already have it." Cory's voice dropped to a whisper and he tapped his lips with his finger in a hushing motion. "Shhh, don't tell anyone but I was doing little Natalie. Lyle wasn't taking care of business if you know what I mean, so I saw my chance. She's one hot number, our Nat. A wild woman in the sack. Lyle was a lucky man."

Shit and fuck. Now Logan had to talk to Natalie again. He also couldn't believe a word out of her mouth. Everything she'd said was now suspect.

Nothing in this case was easy and it was starting to piss him off.

✧ ✧ ✧ ✧

Natalie was nowhere to be found the next morning. It appeared that she and her friend had followed the advice to take a little vacation; however, they seemed to have forgotten to inform Drake or Tanner when they did it. The two women had slipped out sometime between the deputy checking on them at two and four in the morning.

Logan called Jared and asked him to track their credit cards. It wouldn't take long to locate them. He still didn't think she'd killed Lyle, but she'd left out a major point when questioned so he needed to talk to her again.

His day didn't get any better when he'd found out that Bruce's alibi didn't check out. His fellow Rotary club members didn't remember seeing him at the breakfast. That meant he had to drive out to Bruce's house to talk to his father-in-law. He wasn't there but a helpful neighbor informed him that Bruce was visiting his daughter.

It only took a few minutes to drive from Bruce's house to Mary's. Bruce's car was parked in front of the house when he pulled up, along with Carol's. He didn't really want to have this conversation in front of the entire family. He'd already upset Ava this morning when he'd told her where he was headed. She didn't want to think that her father was capable of this and neither did he. He also didn't have a clue as to how Mary would respond to the latest news. She was unpredictable at the best of times and this certainly wasn't one of them.

Just get it over with.

Striding up to the door, he knocked hoping it would be Bruce that answered. Perhaps he could sneak his father-in-law into the den without Mary and Carol seeing him.

The door swung open and Carol stood on the other side wearing a big, welcoming smile.

"Logan, what a lovely surprise. Come in. I just put on a fresh pot of coffee. Are you alone?"

He followed her into the kitchen where Bruce and Mary were enjoying some of Carol's famous scrambled eggs. "Just me. Ava's home with the kids. They're having a picnic in the backyard. Complete with sandwiches, potato chips, and ants."

Carol laughed as she poured him a cup of coffee. "You can't have a picnic without ants. It wouldn't be right. I was going to give her a call later and invite you all over for dinner tonight. I've had a hankering for lasagna. There'll be enough for an army."

He loved Carol's lasagna which was also Ava's lasagna, but he didn't answer as she might want to rescind his invitation after she heard why he was there. Or maybe not. He kept forgetting that Carol and Bruce were divorcing. This show of solidarity was for Mary and the situation. It wasn't because they longed to spend time with each other.

Logan accepted the steaming cup of java and took a sip. Damn, he needed the caffeine.

"Bruce, do you have a minute?"

His father-in-law gave him a sharp look from his spot at the table. He had to know why Logan wanted to talk to him.

He ate the last bite of his eggs. "I do."

"Maybe we could go into the den?"

Carol's smile was gone and Mary wasn't looking too happy either, but then she rarely did.

"What's going on?" his mother-in-law asked, her gaze going back and forth between Logan and her soon to be ex-husband. "Someone needs to speak up."

Bruce exhaled noisily and took a bite of his toast. "It's okay, Logan. Whatever you have to say, you can say right here. We're all family, after all."

This wasn't what he'd wanted to happen. So very bad.

"About where you were when Lyle was shot…"

In unison, Carol and Mary's heads swiveled toward Bruce who had the grace to look embarrassed.

"What about it?"

Logan took another gulp of the scalding hot coffee, enjoying the burn all the way down to his stomach. "We talked to the other Rotary members there that day and it seems none of them can remember you being there. Do you have any explanation for that?"

"None. I was definitely there."

But invisible?

"We also asked the wait staff and they can't remember you either."

"I doubt they pay much attention."

Bruce wasn't going down without a fight.

"When no one could remember you being there, Drake pulled the traffic light footage from the intersection in front of the restaurant. You would have had to go through there but he didn't see your car."

Folding his hands in front of him, Bruce finally capitulated. "Fine, I wasn't there. I was supposed to be but I didn't feel like going. I went fishing instead."

As explanations went, it was believable. Bruce did fish. He was retired now so he had the flexibility to do whatever he wanted. The Rotary breakfasts were boring as hell most of the time. Half of the old-timers dozed off during the speech. Sometimes the snoring was so loud the speaker had to practically yell.

"Did you go with anyone?"

"No, I went alone. I wanted some peace and quiet with my

own thoughts. And before you ask, no one saw me drive out there. I did stop at the diner on the way back but that was about ten in the morning."

"Did you catch anything?"

"No."

Scraping his hand down his face, Logan groaned. "Help me out here, Bruce. There has to be someone who saw you that morning."

Mary jumped up from the table. "You don't actually believe that Daddy shot Lyle? That's crazy."

"It doesn't matter what I believe," Logan explained as patiently as possible. "It only matters what the prosecutor and a jury believe. Your father had a motive, although not the strongest one. I'm trying to clear him from the list of suspects. The sooner we get him – and you, for that matter – off of that list, the better off we'll be. Then I can concentrate on finding the real killer."

Carol busied herself cleaning up the dirty dishes, clearly disturbed that Bruce was lying. Again.

Crossing her arms over her chest, Mary stared Logan down. "If you had any family loyalty you wouldn't bother with us. You'd go out there and find the man that shot my husband."

Logan was getting fucking tired of people lecturing him about family loyalty. He could have run in Mary and Bruce for questioning at the station multiple times but he hadn't done that.

Family loyalty.

The words always made him think of the Brysons. At one time there had been the three brothers and then Logan. Wade had gone to prison and Lyle had been shot. That left Logan and Aaron.

Aaron. He'd heard little from the middle brother since coming to town. Where had Aaron been that morning? He had a motive now when he hadn't at first. Lyle was bleeding Bryson money right and left. Did Aaron even know? Honestly, the true state of Bryson finances was still a mystery Ava was diligently working on.

"You're right, Mary. Talking to you is a waste of time."

He turned on his heel and headed for the door.

"Where are you going?" Mary asked, trailing after him. Just seconds ago she hadn't wanted him to leave and now she didn't seem to want him to go.

"To see your brother-in-law," he replied with a grin. "I need to find out what Aaron knew and when he knew it."

CHAPTER TWENTY-SIX

Rubbing her tired eyes, Ava lifted her arms over her head and stretched her stiff back muscles. She'd been sitting for far too long. The twins were busy playing in a blanket fort she'd built them about an hour ago. The only sounds coming from the chair reinforced structure were giggles and whispers. They'd taken every stuffed animal they'd brought from home in there with them as well, and it sounded as if they were playing school. Brianna loved telling everyone what to do and Colt enjoyed it as well. Whether the stuffies were taking direction was an open question, however. Brianna was always saying her teddy bear liked to be naughty and needed frequent timeouts.

Ava had been staring at Bryson Construction financial documents since the day before and she was beginning to go slightly stir crazy. Nothing seemed out of place. Not really. Expenses were high but their revenue was steady thanks to a stream of jobs from one particular customer. They weren't making tons of money but they were keeping their head above water. Lyle and Aaron were able to pay themselves every two weeks, although they weren't pulling down what some might call an executive salary. The fact that Lyle and Mary were spending it as fast as they made it wasn't the fault of the corporation.

"Mom, can we have cookies?"

Ava looked up from her documents to the face of her six-year-old daughter. Brianna had a huge sweet tooth which she'd inherited from Logan. He had the metabolism to burn off every calorie he consumed and then some. It looked like the children did too, but that didn't mean Ava was going to hand out cookies on a whim.

"It's too close to dinnertime. You'll spoil your supper."

I have become my mother. I remember her saying the exact same words.
I swore I wouldn't do it to my kids. Yet here I am.
I could use a cookie.
I'd have to eat in the bathroom or pantry. Behind a locked door.

"Just one," Brianna sighed. "I promise I'll eat my peas."

"How do you know we're having peas?"

"There's hamburger in the refrigerator. That means peas."

Ava usually made cheeseburgers with peas on the side. It made her feel less guilty that she'd made red meat for dinner.

I'm becoming predictable. Maybe Logan is bored with cheeseburgers and peas.

"No, sweetheart. We really are going to eat dinner in a little while. I'm going to take a break in about fifteen minutes and start cooking."

Brianna leaned forward so her elbows were on the table and she was balanced on her tiptoes.

"Whatcha doing?"

Educating the children that law enforcement wasn't all shoot 'em up and car chases seemed like an excellent idea.

"I'm combing through these financial papers trying to see if anything looks unusual."

Brianna studied the paper on the top of the pile as if she understood profit and loss. Perhaps she did. She was growing up too fast. Logan was right. Six going on sixteen.

"Did you find anything?"

"Not yet. Everything looks like it should. Good customers who pay on time. The ideal scenario."

Good customers who pay on time. Hmmm...

The six-year-old attention span was small. Brianna was already bored.

"Can I help you make dinner? Can we eat in the fort?"

Brianna liked to shape the burgers. She did a pretty good job, too.

"Absolutely. I need my number one helper. I'll call you when it's time. And sure, you can eat in the fort. But you have to eat all your peas."

Her daughter bounded away and back under the blanket without agreeing to the deal. Green vegetables were always a fight. Carrots and potatoes went over much more easily.

Good customers who pay on time. Ideal.

One customer that seemed too good to be true. Every month they had a large influx of business and they paid on time. Never one day late. Every business should have such a wonderful client.

Ava dug through the pile and pulled out all the folders that dealt with Timber Ridge Development. There were no details on the company but that wasn't a problem. She knew just who to call. She punched a few buttons on her phone and lifted it to her ear.

"Jared? Hi, it's Ava. I'm helping Logan with the Bryson case and I was hoping you could look up a corporation for me. Timber Ridge Development. No, I don't know where they were incorporated but they're Bryson Construction's biggest customer by at least ten times. I don't know what we're looking for I'm just doing a Logan thing and following my gut. They're almost too good to be true. Without them, Bryson Construction would have been out of business a year ago. You will? Thanks, I owe you."

It was probably another dead end. They'd had too many of those lately.

If Logan lived to be a hundred and four, he'd never understand the Bryson family. Their logic was clearly beyond his comprehension. They made absolutely no fucking sense.

"So you knew Lyle was losing money? That he was in debt to his eyeballs?"

Aaron sat at his desk across from Logan who had taken up pacing back and forth in the small space. The other man looked completely unperturbed about the entire subject as if Lyle's gambling addiction was no big deal and that Logan was overreacting.

"I knew but we were dealing with that internally." Aaron leaned forward, his palms flat on the desk. "Like a family. The way things should be done."

"Internally," Logan echoed. "Just how were you dealing with it? You didn't get Lyle to stop gambling and seeing another woman."

Red suffused Aaron's cheeks and he cleared his throat a few times. "His relationship with Mary was his own business. He never brought his girlfriend into work so I didn't stick my nose where it didn't belong."

"Fine, you didn't care that he had a side piece and you didn't care that he was gambling all his money and *your* money away. You're a great brother, Aaron. Not many would be so accommodating. You just didn't give a shit that he was bankrupting your company. Are you taking Valium or something? Or is it meditation? Just how do you stay so calm?"

"Bryson Construction is hardly bankrupt. We may not be cash rich but we've made payroll every single week. We also never miss a payment to our suppliers."

That was true. Ava had been able to ascertain that quickly from the stack of financial statements on the kitchen table.

"Let's talk about assets then."

"What about them?"

"Do you have any? According to Natalie, Lyle was going to pay his bookie back with Bryson assets but he needed to do it in a way that you wouldn't know."

Aaron was shaking his head before Logan finished. "There isn't any way to do that. When Wade…left…we made it so both of us have to sign off on any sales or major contracts. He couldn't get rid of anything without my agreement and vice versa."

Logan's phone vibrated in his pocket and with a growl of frustration he pulled it out, reading the long text from his wife.

I'm going to give her a big kiss when I get home.

He tucked the phone away in his pocket. "So let me get this straight. Neither of you can sell anything without the other agreeing to it. You also can't enter into any business deals without the other's say so. Is that about right?"

"That's right. So he couldn't use Bryson assets to pay off his debt without my knowledge. Natalie was wrong."

"You're right. She was," Logan agreed, settling into a guest chair and stretching out his legs. "What can you tell me about Timber Ridge Development?"

The once smiling and relaxed Aaron paled slightly and shifted in his chair. "They're a customer of ours."

"Your biggest customer. By far. In fact, without them you'd

OLIVIA JAYMES

be bankrupt."

"We're very lucky they came along when they did."

Logan nodded, stroking his chin. "About a year ago, right? Just about when Lyle got into major debt trouble. Funny on that timing."

"I'm not sure when we first started doing work for Timber Ridge."

Logan tapped his denim clad thighs. "Funny thing about them. They're owned by a holding company in Canada. So Jared did a little more digging and found a string of holding companies that all come back to one family. The Eldridge family. As in Cory Eldridge, owner of the nightclub and gambling den where Lyle owes his money. Isn't that a strange coincidence?"

Logan sat up straight, a smile finally turning up the corners of his lips. "More fun facts. Cory Eldridge's uncle did some federal time for racketeering back in the nineties and his dad has been under scrutiny by the ATF for years. Interesting people you do business with."

Aaron's throat bobbed and all color had drained from his face. "I didn't–I didn't know any of that."

Logan stood and leaned over the desk so he and Aaron were almost nose to nose. Beads of sweat had broken out on Aaron's forehead. "Let me guess how this went down. Lyle got ass deep in debt and couldn't pay it back. The company barely has any assets so he couldn't sell anything. You weren't willing to part with any personal assets so he didn't have much choice. He could get his kneecaps removed and his bones broken or he could launder drug and gambling money through Bryson Construction for the Eldridge family. The only question I have is when did you find out? Did you know from the beginning or did you find out later?"

Aaron reached into the pocket of his blazer and pulled out a

176

white handkerchief, dabbing at his face. "I didn't know. Not at first."

"But you figured it out eventually."

Aaron nodded, looking close to tears. "I couldn't let my brother be hurt. I put the family first—"

"Right," Logan cut in. "Loyalty and all that jazz. Even if it's illegal."

"So what does this mean?"

The question came out squeaky and high pitched. He was scared and he should be. He could do some hard time for this.

"I'll leave the money laundering to Drake and the Feds. That isn't my problem. As for your motive, well, you didn't really have one since you knew about the debt and didn't think it was a problem. Eldridge loses his motive as well because he wouldn't want to lose the mechanism for getting his money clean. It doesn't help Mary or Bruce however. They still have motive – and right now – rotten alibis."

A tear squeezed out of Aaron's eye and slid down his cheek. "Mary didn't do it. I know for a certainty."

For a moment Logan almost turned his back and walked out. This family was a pimple on the ass of society.

"And how do you know that?" Logan asked with a heavy sigh. He was going to hate the answer. There was no doubt about that.

"She was at our house. Lindsay and I had a bad argument and she called Mary to come over and get her. She was planning on packing up and leaving. Then of course the whole thing with Lyle blew up so she didn't."

"Why didn't she tell me this?"

"Because I asked her not to," Aaron admitted. "I didn't want anyone to know how things had gotten between me and Lindsey."

Snapping his teeth together, Logan held back the words he really wanted to say.

"Drake may want to add obstruction of justice to your charges. Is there anything else that I don't know?"

"No, nothing." Aaron shrugged as if the entire incident was no big deal. "Not a thing."

Logan didn't believe him but for now he had to accept the answer.

CHAPTER TWENTY-SEVEN

The twins happily went into the family room to watch cartoons for a few minutes while Ava talked to her husband. Logan had just pulled into the driveway and she was pacing back and forth in front of the door, half angry and half happy. It was a strange combination to feel all at once and it had her pulse racing and her heart pounding in her ears.

She didn't know whether to kiss Logan or yell at him. Heck, she might do both. In fact, she was sure she was going to do both of those things and a few others as well.

The door swung open and Logan came inside, a grim expression on his face. He'd had a crappy day and it wasn't her intention to make it worse but dammit, this couldn't wait.

Stopping short when he saw that she was standing right in front of him, he leaned down to greet her with a kiss.

"Hey, honey. Is that cheeseburgers I smell?"

"It is." She took his beat up brown leather briefcase out of his hands and placed it on the foyer table. "Is there anything you want to tell me, my darling husband?"

Like a deer in headlights, Logan froze. "Why do you ask?"

Ava walked toward the kitchen beckoning to her spouse.

This wasn't a discussion for the house entrance. "I had the most interesting discussion with Jason today. Jared was caught up in a meeting so he couldn't call me back with the Timber Ridge details. Jason called instead. Do you know what he asked me?"

Her husband was beginning to relax, a smile playing on his lips. "Jason ratted me out, didn't he?"

Logan thought this was funny. *Funny.*

He was going to be walking funny when she was done with him.

"Ratted you out? That's all you have to say for yourself? Your business partner asked me if I was happy that you wouldn't be traveling anymore. Imagine my surprise when I heard this."

Leaning a hip against the kitchen counter, Logan was wearing his trademark grin. "I was saving it for a surprise but I guess it's official. Kim hadn't decided for sure to stick with the firm. She's a city girl and let's face it, most of the assignments are in little piss ant towns like this one. I didn't want to raise your hopes only to have to tell you it wasn't happening."

Kim? What did she have to do with this?

"Wait...what? How does Kim fit into this equation?"

Crap, was she going to be working even more closely with Logan?

I cannot catch a break.

Logan was looking at her as if she was pretty but not very bright. "Kim is going to take my position in the firm, traveling as a hands-on consultant. I'm taking a different role in the firm providing computer and data expertise along with a managerial role for our support staff. Jared is going to specialize in some of the more...shall we say darker aspects of research, while I concentrate on the myriad of requests that come in every day. Jared desperately needs the help and the office in Seattle is growing by leaps and bounds. It needs someone to man the helm, so to speak. That's why I've been spending so much time with Kim. I needed to first evaluate her level of skill and then get her trained up so she could take over."

Falling back into a kitchen chair, Ava rested her head in her hands. "I want to kiss you and kick you in the balls. I'm going to do both but I'm not sure which I'm going to do first."

Laughing, Logan playfully covered his crotch with his hands. "Baby, I think you like what I got going on here. Think before you do that."

She looked up at her husband. So handsome. So sexy. So full of shit. He made her crazy and he ought to thank the good heavens that she was in love with him.

"I had no idea of what was going on, you idiot. I thought we were at the point in our marriage where you liked working more than being home. I thought...maybe...Kim was more interesting. I mean...she catches criminals better than I do."

"Because that's my criteria when it comes to choosing a mate for life? And you are stuck with me for life, good girl. Don't think I'm ever going to let you go. And just so you know...I was beginning to think that maybe you preferred it when I was gone."

He had to have lost his mind. She wasn't planning to go anywhere nor was she planning to let him wander away either.

"You rarely call me *good girl* anymore." She raised her hands up when he would have reached for her. "And I'm still pissed at you. If you'd have just told me this would have gone a lot smoother."

He leaned down so his hands were resting on his knees and their noses were almost touching. "I am sorry about that. I just wanted it to be a sure thing before I told you. And as for not calling you good girl? That's because it doesn't fit so much. We've done some pretty naughty things in the bedroom, baby.

While I can definitely say that you were *good* at it, I cannot say that you're a good girl if that adjective means that you don't get down and dirty with your man."

Glancing over her shoulder, Ava wanted to make sure that the children were still glued to the television. They didn't need to hear their father talking like this to their mother.

"You're not so bad yourself, handsome."

"But I am." His lips pressed against hers and his tongue ran along her bottom lip. "A bad boy. Just ask your dad. He'll tell you."

Rolling her eyes, she pulled him back in for another kiss. "I don't think my father has a leg to stand on when it comes to opinions about you. Are you really going to be home more?"

Logan's answer was to wrap his arms around her waist and lift her out of the chair and onto the kitchen counter. Her legs were splayed so he could fit snugly between them. They couldn't start anything, but it sure gave her ideas about things they could do after the kids were in bed.

"I'm going to be home so much you're going to get thoroughly sick of me." He cocked his head to one side. "Did you honestly think I found Kim more interesting than you? Baby, you are the most fascinating woman I've ever met, and you certainly keep me on my toes. Every day with you is more fun than the day before."

Now he was just being silly. Every day couldn't possibly be like that. But she might just be that fascinating. At least to him.

"You and she have a lot in common. She's caught some nasty criminals."

"So have you. Whether real or literary. You have to know that I love you."

"I do know, and I know that you're devoted to us. My jealousy didn't make any sense and I knew that. I guess it was that she seemed to get all the best time with you. When you were home you were tired or distracted. She got…prime time…and I got what was left over. I think that's why I was feeling down." Ava didn't know if she was doing a good job of explaining this. "As much as you've hated being here in Corville, I got to spend so much time with you. Work with you. I've missed that. Sometimes it feels like we're on parallel paths that rarely cross."

Rubbing his lips across hers, he whispered the words that always made her heart skip a beat.

"Baby, you're the one. The only one. Forever." He pulled back and looked into her eyes. She could feel the emotion radiating off of him, that passion and fervor she'd never take for granted. "I'm going to do better. I don't want you to have even one moment of doubt."

She couldn't let him take the rap for this. It was all her own insecurities. She'd known they were stupid but she'd let them worm their way into her brain, making her think things that made no sense.

"It's not your fault. This is my issue."

"We do things as a couple so it's our issue. You know, I get a little insecure, too. I've often thought that you and the kids were such a tight unit. You go about your daily business and handle everything just fine without me. You don't…really need me."

How could this man possibly think that? She needed him all of the time.

"I must be a heck of an actress," Ava declared with a smile. "Because I need and miss you all the time. Sure, I can take out the garbage and kill the spiders by myself but it's after the kids are in bed and I'm all alone. That's when I need you most of all."

"I hope you mean that because I'm going to be home pretty much every night from now on."

Ava couldn't think of anything she wanted more. It sounded like heaven.

"I suppose you think you're going to get lucky more often," she teased. "But there won't be any more going away sex or welcome home sex."

She didn't mention the stuff they did on the phone or Skype. That was the I-miss-you-sex.

His lips found that special spot right underneath her ear and she almost melted into a pool of goo on the granite countertop.

"I think I'm lucky just being your husband, but I guess you could say that I'm looking forward to a lot more...togetherness. In fact, let's start right now."

"The kids are watching cartoons in the other room," she reminded him. "They only get a few hours a day of screen time and it's not even dinner yet. Can you wait until we put them to bed?"

She moaned the last part of her sentence, her pulse thrumming in private places. He was far too good with that tongue and those fingers. She wasn't sure she could wait to be honest.

"I can wait, good girl, but be prepared to be very bad tonight."

It was good to have him home.

CHAPTER TWENTY-EIGHT

The next night Ava, Logan, Drake, and Tanner all sat around the coffee table nibbling at the remains of the pizza. Logan and Drake sat on the floor while Tanner and Ava sat on the couch and the chair. The twins were tucked up in bed after having been read a whopping six stories. Three by Ava, one by Logan, another by Drake, and the last by Tanner. They were now sleeping peacefully with a tummy full of sausage and cheese.

Tanner bit into a piece of crust. "We're back at square one. Mary, Aaron, and his wife Lindsay alibi for each other, plus the neighbors remember the loud argument. We were also able to place Mary's vehicle on the road to their house that morning with a traffic camera so that corroborates their story. Drake found a witness to your father-in-law's fishing so he's out. Cory Eldridge no longer has a motive either because he would have wanted to keep his good money laundering scheme going. So now we've got bupkiss."

Ava snorted. "We'd be lucky to get bupkiss. No one has a motive or if they do they have an alibi."

Drake steepled his fingers and rested his chin on them. "What do we do now? Are we saying that it was some random event? A serial killer or maybe a hunter that wasn't paying attention?"

"I hope that no one was hunting in the local park," Logan replied, his own expression sober. The whole case was at a standstill. While Ava was thrilled her sister and father were innocent she'd hoped for the evidence to send her off onto a productive path. That hadn't happened. They were stuck in quicksand. "As for a serial killer, that's a theory but what are the chances of two serial killers in a town this small? I'm no math genius but the odds have to be astronomical."

Ava agreed but this entire case had been strange. "I think you're right about the math but we have to consider the possibility. No one else has been killed but that doesn't mean anything. If we can't find Lyle's shooter, then we need to be cognizant when future crimes are investigated. They might be related."

"Has Jared done a search for similar crimes?" Tanner queried. "Maybe the killer was passing through."

"He did," Logan confirmed. "He didn't find anything that tripped my radar. We do have to think about the possibility that this was an accident. Someone playing with a gun – maybe a kid – and it went off by accident. Lyle was in the wrong place at the wrong time."

Tanner didn't look convinced. "What's your gut telling you?"

Logan was famous for his lawman gut. It had solved more crimes than the heroes in Ava's mystery novels.

"It wasn't an accident. Someone shot Lyle, but who or why I don't know."

Logan was trying to play it off but Ava knew her husband too well. He was pained terribly that he couldn't solve this crime. He didn't like it when he thought a criminal was smarter than he was. With his personal connection to the victim, she didn't see him simply walking away and moving on to the next case either.

"That leaves us sitting here eating pizza," Drake said glumly. "The only thing I know to do is go back over the evidence we already have."

"What would your characters do, Ava?" Tanner said with a laugh. "Who would be the killer in one of your books?"

"That's an easy question. The killer is always the person it absolutely couldn't be."

"And who is that?" Drake asked.

"Wade," Logan replied between gritted teeth. "That would be Wade."

It couldn't be Wade. That was impossible.

The silence stretched on as everyone contemplated Logan's words. It didn't make any sense but little had in this case.

"It can't be Wade," Ava argued, sitting up on the couch. "He's in prison. He couldn't have shot Lyle. And he doesn't have a motive either."

"He hates the Bryson family's brand of loyalty," Logan said. "He told me that when I visited him. And he sure as shit wasn't all broken up about his little brother's death, not that I expected him to be. He's grown a hell of a lot colder since being inside. But I will say that he had nothing but contempt for the Bryson business dealings."

"But he couldn't have done it." Drake looked around the group. "Right?"

Tanner's eyes narrowed as he watched Logan closely. "What've you got on your mind? You're thinking something. I can practically see the hamster wheels turning in your head. Talk to us."

Logan sat up and leaned on one hand, his legs stretched out on the rug. "Wade made a big deal about telling me that he's like a king inside. He's got people who look up to him, he's got female groupies outside that want to marry him and have his baby. Do you think that one of those women would kill for him?"

Ava's curiosity was piqued. "Do you think Wade was trying to brag without actually admitting to anything?"

"Wade is a sick individual," Logan reminded her with a grimace. "He's not dealing with reality, especially behind bars. He has his own little world there and apparently he's a worshipped like a god. But I think we should get a look at Wade's visitor logs. According to Aaron he won't see his family but he might see some of his admirers. We could check out the names."

"We need to check his mail, too," Tanner added. "These serial killers get a ton of mail from lovelorn ladies. We need to check the ones he writes to. He's got a lot of free time on his hands. He might be pen pals with several people."

Logan looked happier than he had a few minutes ago. "I'll check with the prison tomorrow. Drake, we may need a warrant."

"I'll get it," Drake vowed, already pulling his phone from his pocket. "I'll call the county judge and get him to sign off on it tonight."

They had a direction to go in. A new start.

Had Wade conspired to have his younger brother killed? It was a long shot of a theory but they had to check it out.

CHAPTER TWENTY-NINE

L ogan and Drake were clearly unwelcome guests in Dr. Marilyn Bartlett's office. Annoyed that she'd had to move appointments around to accommodate them and their court order, she still greeted them politely when they showed up at the prison the next day.

Like the last time he'd met with her, her office was only marginally more colorful and happy than the rest of the institution. Her gray walls were decorated with diplomas and her desk had that same sad little potted plant but that was the extent of the personalization. As before, she was dressed in a navy blue skirt and blazer and the same shoes with the sensible heel. He couldn't help but wonder how many of those blue suits and shoes she had at home in her wardrobe.

Dr. Bartlett pointed to two boxes of letters that were stacked next to her desk. The boxes were large and heavy, indicating that there were far too many lonely and troubled women out there who would write to a convicted serial killer.

"The boxes contain the incoming mail. Wade hasn't answered many letters," the psychologist said, lifting a thick folder from a drawer in the filing cabinet. "We scan and read all outgoing mail. These are copies of all of his correspondence outside of the prison. I doubt you'll find anything interesting in there. Nor will you find anything of substance in his incoming letters. I've read them all and they're harmless."

"What about his visitors?" Logan asked. "Have any of the women come to visit him? We'd like to get a copy of his visitor logs."

Dr. Bartlett shook her head. "Sadly, you won't find them helpful either. He's had few visitors. He refuses most of them. He allowed his family at first but then no one except his attorney. You're the first in a long time, Mr. Wright. I'm hoping that's a sign that he's perhaps turned a corner and is becoming more social."

This woman was an optimist. An unsmiling, rigid, chilly optimist.

"We'd still like a copy," Drake replied, tapping the signed court order they'd placed on the good doctor's desk. "We'll wait."

"No need," Dr. Bartlett said dismissively. "I assumed that you would want them. I pulled everything together when I received your message this morning. I was simply trying to save you some work. You won't get any help from his visitor history. The logs are already in the box."

This woman was so cold she ought to be followed around by a parade of penguins. "You don't think much of our theory."

She made a small shrugging motion with her shoulder. "It's not for me to say. You're the law enforcement officers. I have no experience there. My job is to aid in the rehabilitation of prisoners. When that isn't possible I help them learn to modify their behavior so they can function behind these walls."

"But you do have experience with troubled, lost people," Logan pressed. "You can't say that there isn't a history of women helping men in prison."

"A small history. It seems like more because it makes the news. But it makes the news, Mr. Wright, because it's a rather rare occurrence. That doesn't mean that you aren't correct, however. There absolutely could be someone out there who wanted Wade Bryson's approval. Who might kill to please him."

"Wade would certainly love that."

She folded her hands together and placed them on the desk. "I've been working with Wade Bryson for over five years now and I hope he's moved past that point. He has made progress."

Logan didn't want to burst the woman's bubble but that was bullshit. She probably had to believe that to be able to come in here every day and do her job, but Wade was no better than the day Logan had arrested him. He might even be worse, if it was possible. He'd been bragging about being worshipped by people. That sounded like the same old Wade who had wanted to be a hero and catch criminals. Nothing had really changed, only the venue.

"That's good to hear," Logan said, not wanting to rock the boat. She'd been very cooperative about them basically messing up her day. "We need more dedicated individuals such as yourself in the criminal justice system."

He could say that with total truth. They did need more people like Marilyn Bartlett. Many more. Wade was a lost cause but there were others on the inside who just needed a helping hand and someone who cared.

For a moment Logan thought he saw the wisp of a smile. Maybe she wasn't so frosty after all. She probably had to act that way in here just to get any respect.

"Please let me know if there's anything I can do to help your investigation. As I said, I don't think you'll find anything in those letters but I hope that I'm wrong."

"We really do appreciate your help." Logan hefted one of the boxes under his arm. "I'm sorry that we didn't give you more notice."

Dr. Bartlett stood and nodded. "Thank you. Will you be visiting Wade Bryson again, Mr. Wright?"

Would he? An interesting question that he hadn't thought about until now.

"Maybe. I need to do more research but there is a possibility. Why do you ask?"

"To prepare him. After your last visit, Wade acted out during dinner. He spent a few days in solitary."

Drake frowned. "I thought you said you were hopeful that he was progressing?"

"Progression doesn't happen in a straight line. The fact that Wade expressed any emotion at all after seeing Mr. Wright is a huge step in the right direction. Now he needs to work on showing emotion in an acceptable way. Two steps forward, one step back."

Logan didn't want to make her job any harder than it already was. "I promise to contact you if I need to speak with him again. How does that sound?"

Another almost smile. Heck, she might be thawing toward him a little.

"That's very kind of you. Thank you. Can I get someone to help you with the boxes?"

Shaking his head, Drake hefted the second box under his arm. "Thank you, Doctor, but we've got this."

Did they have it? A clue that could finally move this case forward? Logan was as hopeful as he'd been since arriving in Corville. He had a good feeling about this.

Chapter Thirty

A va needed a shower. And a scrub brush with a strong disinfectant. And hot, hot water. *Ewww.*

Reading these letters to Wade Bryson made her feel incredibly dirty and not in a good way. The women – and some of the men – hadn't held back and had written in vivid detail what they wanted to do to Wade should they ever have the opportunity. Or a conjugal visit.

Wade hadn't been exaggerating. He had a whole contingent of people who loved him, but so far, none were willing to kill for him. She'd been sitting at the kitchen table reading letters the better part of the afternoon and evening, only taking a break to eat dinner with the family. She'd just placed the last one back in the box. Definitely creeped out, but she hadn't found much for them to run with. In fact, it looked like they'd come up with a great big goose egg.

They were once again back to square one. They had nothing and no one.

Logan was in the living room playing a game of *Go Fish* with Brianna and Colt while Ava worked. He'd already read Wade's own outgoing mail and the doctor was correct in saying it appeared completely innocuous. He was his usual audacious and bragging self, enjoying being fawned over by a female but there was nothing in there that looked like it might set off one of his followers to do deadly deeds.

If anything, they were almost all the same, generic really. He didn't ask them anything personal. Mostly he wrote about himself and how he was simply misunderstood, but a good man deep down. He'd been trying to help law enforcement but his efforts had been twisted and bastardized.

Wade didn't seem to care about these women as people. They simply existed to orbit him like the sun. And he never mentioned his family. Not once.

The incoming letters were much more disturbing, of course. From both men and women, these were people that clearly had issues in their life. The fact that they'd zeroed in on a serial killer as the one person that could understand them left Ava shaking her head.

Some of the letters were from people who admired Wade. They wanted to be like him and sought his counsel.

That's disturbing as hell. We need to look at these people.

Some of the letters were from lovelorn women who were sure all Wade needed was the love of a good woman and he wouldn't ever want to kill again. It was in this stack that she'd found the icky ones that made her feel dirty. And more than a few nude photos.

Some of the letters wanted something personal of Wade's to sell online. They were simply businesspeople who made money off of serial killer groupies.

Three words that shouldn't even go together. Serial killer groupies. WTF?

There were, however, no offers to kill on Wade's behalf. No inquiries about the Bryson family. Those disturbed enough to ask for advice appeared to be more worried about the people *they* wanted to kill rather than anyone Wade might want dead.

He also hadn't followed up with any of these letter-writers. Some had written multiple times but had eventually given up. Wade might like admirers but he didn't want to take the time to write them back.

She was packing up the boxes and placing them on the floor when Logan joined her in the kitchen.

"All done? Did you find anything?"

Wrinkling her nose, she shook her head. "Nothing. There's nothing here, although after reading these letters I weep for humanity. What have we come to as a society?"

Logan poured out milk into two plastic glasses before snagging a beer for himself.

"That's a small sliver of the population, babe. There have always been troubled people throughout history. We just get to see more of them with our occupations."

"Aren't we a glass half-full kind of guy tonight."

He held up his beer bottle. "More like a bottle full. Are you coming out to play with us? Brianna, the little card shark, is beating the pants off of me and Colt."

"She wins a lot."

"Does she cheat?"

"Logan Wright, what a terrible thing to say about your own daughter." Ava laughed at his expression. "And in answer to your question, yes, I think she does cheat. You have to watch her closely. I've caught her trying to look at mine or Colt's cards. Have you been paying attention?"

"I will now," Logan declared chuckling. "Damn, she must really like to win."

"She gets that from you."

"Yeah, because winning means nothing to you. Seriously, are

you coming out into the living room? I could use the help. It's two against one out there."

There was no point in beating the proverbial dead horse. She'd been through all the letters and while she'd seen some severely disturbed individuals she wouldn't want to meet in a dark alley – or anywhere else, for that matter – none of them had offered to do Wade's bidding. She had set aside a few letters to check out though simply because they gave her the willies when she read them. Someone needed to look into those people and make sure they hadn't acted on their homicidal tendencies.

"I'll help you if you pop some popcorn."

Logan threw back his head and laughed. "That's it? That's all you want? Just some butter and salt drenched kernels."

"No, I want a gigantic bowl full of them."

He bowed low and gave her a playful wink. "Your wish is my command."

She insinuated her fingers underneath the hem of his t-shirt and stroked the flesh that stretched across his washboard abs. "Oh yeah? I've got a few commands for later then."

"If we're naked, I'm totally on board."

Sliding her hands up his torso, she then wrapped her arms around his lean waist and rested her head on his chest. This felt so amazingly good. Close to her husband, his warm familiar scent, the heavy and reassuring thud of his heartbeat under her cheek.

"I can make that happen."

"Is this because I'm going to be home more?"

She looked up into his crystal blue gaze. "I'd be all over your fine self no matter what but it doesn't hurt."

"You're pretty hot too, good girl."

A shiver always ran through her at his endearment. It re-minded her of…the old days. When she'd wondered if she would ever be able to take this tiger and turn him into a housecat.

Turns out the answer is no. But I don't care. I wouldn't have him any other way.

"Thank you, though. I could say that the kids are going to be thrilled but I am, too. You're the only one that I want making me insane for the rest of my life."

"Back at you, babe. No one makes me crazier than you do." He leaned down and pressed his lips tenderly to her forehead. "I didn't do it just for you. I did it for me. I was missing far too much in our lives. I felt like a ghost in my own family."

It had been like that. He'd haunted their home but he hadn't ever been truly there. That was going to change and she couldn't be more thrilled.

Except...it didn't feel right that the last case he led ended like this. He should be going out with a blaze of glory. This felt more like a whimper of defeat.

The question had been bugging her all evening as her hope had faded. Was Logan ready to give up?

It was a question that only he could answer. Did she dare ask it?

"So...what now?"

He backed away and reached for his beer. "I'm not sure what you mean."

Five or six years ago she might have bought that answer but she knew better now. His fingers were twitchy, drumming a pattern on the counter. He was avoiding her question.

"You know what I mean. Where do we go from here?"

He didn't answer for a long time and she stayed quiet, letting him gather his thoughts. This was his investigation and he got to make the call when he'd had enough.

"I don't know," he eventually said, his voice soft. "Lyle deserves to have his killer found but I've dug through every lead I can find. There's nothing there. I think I'm going to call Jason and tell him that he should assign someone else. Someone better."

Her husband was so silly sometimes.

"There isn't anyone better. Jason and Jared would say the same thing. If you can't find this person, I doubt anyone can."

He gave her a crooked grin. "You have to say that because you're married to me."

"I'm not saying it because you're my husband. I'm saying it because it's true. If they assign someone else what are they going to do? They're going to go through the evidence that we've already been through a dozen times or more."

"They might see something we didn't."

She couldn't deny the possibility. Fresh eyes could make the world of difference. Perhaps this was one case that needed a new perspective. It was still sad though that Logan hadn't cracked the case. He didn't like losing any more than their daughter did.

This case was personal. Everything with the Bryson family and especially Wade was deeply intimate for him. It brought up memories that he didn't want to deal with. Yet, despite all of that he'd come back here and worked on Lyle's murder.

Because he felt like it was the right thing to do. The people of Corville would never understand Logan Wright. Not truly. They blamed him for the passing of an era when they should thank him for weeding out a remorseless killer.

"Are you okay with this?"

The man she loved was no quitter but he also wasn't about to keep banging his head against a wall and make zero progress.

"Fuck no, I am not okay with it. But I'm going to be eventually. I tried my best and I couldn't get the job done. It happens, babe."

Just not to you, my love.

Ava had to blink back the tears as her heart squeezed tight in her chest. She could feel the pain Logan was in as if she had a real physical wound. He couldn't hide the conflict in his eyes, the tension in his jaw. He wasn't fine with this.

But there were other cases and clients. He couldn't spend forever here.

They had a life to get back to. The kids would be starting school soon and summer was almost over. Corville would get back to normal, too.

She just couldn't let him go out like this. Not with this case.

"How about tomorrow morning I drop the twins at Mom's house and you and me...we hunker down with the evidence. One last time." She placed her hand on his jaw, letting her fingers brush the stubble there. "Just so we can say we did everything we could."

His slow smile was her answer. "Babe, I think that's a great idea. I'll even pick up a frozen pizza."

One more time. They couldn't give up. Not yet.

CHAPTER THIRTY-ONE

L ogan was having a particularly pleasant dream while wrapped around Ava when his phone rudely interrupted his beauty sleep. Without opening his eyes, he reached behind him and felt around on the bedside table until he located the offending piece of technology. Ava stirred in his arms but he gently kissed her cheek. It was time to get up anyway. The twins would be anxious for breakfast in about half an hour.

"Go back to sleep, baby," he murmured in her ear. "It's my phone. Probably work."

She seemed to understand and simply wound up more tightly in the blankets. Slipping out of bed, he placed the phone against his ear and hurried out of the bedroom hoping his wife would easily go back to sleep. The screen displayed a photo of his partner Jason who must have been having another bout of insomnia.

"You better have a damn good reason for calling me this early in the morning."

"Sadly, I do. Sorry about waking you up but I knew you'd want to know right away."

Dressed in only his boxers, Logan headed straight for the

kitchen and the coffeemaker. He and Ava had a busy day ahead of them and caffeine was going to be a requirement.

"Know what? Is everyone okay?"

It was rare but sometimes a consultant was injured while working a case.

"Everyone's fine," Jason assured him. "But I just got a call from an old buddy, a journalist. I used to help him out on occasion and this morning he returned the favor. It hasn't been made public yet, and officials are trying to keep it quiet, but Wade Bryson broke out of prison last night. There's a massive manhunt underway. It's going to make the news eventually, of course, but they're hoping to catch him quickly and quietly."

Logan had to replay Jason's words in his head several times before he could make heads or tails of them. He'd had no coffee and was still half asleep but the words *Wade* and *broke out of prison* had been said in the same sentence.

Words he'd never thought he would hear, frankly. He'd sort of assumed Wade was tucked up safely and would never see freedom again. He was someone they didn't need to worry about. Out of the equation and very much not Logan's problem.

Logan finally found his voice. "Broke out of prison? How the fuck did he do that? No, wait. Don't tell me. He just waltzed out in front of God and everybody. That would be just his way."

Jason chuckled on the other end of the line. "That would be just his way, wouldn't it? But that's not quite how it happened. Right now, they think he snuck out inside a supplier's truck."

"Don't they fucking count heads or something? Didn't anyone notice he was gone?"

Having visited that prison twice in a short period of time, Logan could attest that the security measures appeared solid but then he'd only seen a portion of them.

"He was supposed to be in a session with the prison shrink

last night after he mouthed off to a guard during dinner. That's the last he was seen."

Logan heartily wished that the coffeemaker would hurry the hell up. "Are you telling me that Wade Bryson has been on the run since last night at dinnertime? And they're trying to keep it quiet? Christ."

"He has, and they won't be able to keep it quiet much longer. I think they'd hoped to catch him quickly, but it didn't happen and now they'll need the public's help to spot him."

His brain was already working on the practicality of Wade's situation. What would he need and when would he need it? And where would he go to get it?

"Wade is smart but I doubt he did this alone," Logan said. "He had to have had some help."

"According to you, he doesn't have any help on the outside," Jason pointed out. "You didn't see anything in the letters and he didn't have any visitors."

That was true.

Except…Wade was seeing the prison psychiatrist regularly. Several times a week, in fact.

And he was supposed to be with her last night when he disappeared.

Dr. Bartlett.

"Maybe his help wasn't from the outside," Logan replied, pissed off at himself that he hadn't seen it long before. "Maybe it was from the inside."

"The inside? You mean a guard helped him?"

Logan had always trusted his gut and it was speaking loud and clear at the moment.

"Jason, try your source again. See if Dr. Marilyn Bartlett showed up for work this morning. My bet is she didn't. She's probably already cleared out her bank accounts and she's on the run. With Wade. I'd also bet money that she's the reason he didn't get put in solitary for mouthing off at the guard last night. That's what would normally happen. I bet she intervened and they were so sick of Wade's shit they let her deal with it. Or she might have even paid off the guard."

Logan wondered whether this had been planned for a long time or if his visit yesterday had prompted the two of them to make a move.

"Jesus," Jason breathed. "You have got to be kidding me."

"Wish I was but I think I'm right. Can you get me into her home? I want to search it. It might hold a clue as to where she and Wade ran off to. I'll also need Jared to start digging up anything he can get on her. It might help us find him."

There was a small silence before Jason replied. "Technically, it's not your problem."

"True," Logan conceded. "But I put him behind bars and that's where he needs to be. Believe me when I say that he's up to no good outside. He's not going to lay low and become a model citizen. He's always believed he was wronged when he was convicted and he loves to kill. It gives him a rush and he hasn't had that for a long time. He won't be able to help himself, especially once he gets started. He could go on a spree and then he's everyone's problem."

I might be the one person in the world who can get inside Wade's head. Scary as shit.

"Let me make some calls. Get a shower if you haven't already had one because I think today is going to suck. I'll call you when I have more details. Logan, I hope you're wrong about the doctor."

"I hope so too, but I'm not."

He just hoped that she was still alive, because Wade wouldn't hesitate to kill her when she'd outlived her usefulness.

CHAPTER THIRTY-TWO

Ava and Logan had dropped the twins with her mother and headed out for Dr. Bartlett's home as soon as they'd both showered. The house was near the prison so they had time to eat their breakfast on the go and discuss what they might find, where Wade might be, and of course what he might be planning to do next.

There were many possibilities and few of them were good news. While many escaped prisoners might lie low and try to keep their nose clean so they wouldn't attract any attention to themselves, Logan seemed positive that Wade wouldn't take that route. He loved attention so he wasn't going to disappear somewhere for years. He'd want to make a splash and get the sensational headlines. The question was how long did they have before his first kill? Who would he target?

Ava checked the directions again on her phone. They should be getting close to the doctor's house.

"What if Dr. Bartlett is home with the flu?"

Logan had already confirmed with Jason's source that the therapist hadn't shown up for work this morning.

"Then we'll fix her some tea and ask her where she thinks he might go. If he ever mentioned anyone or anywhere outside of those walls." Logan glanced at her before returning his eyes to the road. "Are you still worried that Wade might be at her house? I've got the local cops meeting us there."

It had crossed her mind a few times. It wasn't out of the question that Wade would show up at the doctor's residence seeking shelter and assistance, whether willingly or by force.

"I think it's a possibility we need to be ready for. The reason she might not be at work could be that he's holding her hostage."

Logan's jaw tightened and his knuckles turned white on the steering wheel. "To be frank, I don't think she's long for this world either way. If Wade is holed up at her house, he won't think twice about killing her. If he does that, heaven help us because he's going to get addicted to that feeling again. Just like a junkie, he's going to need it over and over, more frequently each time. Once won't be enough."

Ava shuddered as she remembered seeing the body of Wade's own father who he had shot in the head.

"You think he'll go on a spree?"

"I think it's highly likely. He'll love the press coverage."

Ava pointed to a small white house on the corner of a quiet residential street. Jason had already called them back and told them that the local police weren't all that interested in Dr. Marilyn Bartlett if they weren't sure that she had broken any laws. As far as the police were concerned, Logan had an interesting theory but absolutely no evidence.

Luckily Jason was able to convince the local cops to at least meet them there in case the doctor's life was in danger. He'd suggested that they wouldn't want the bad publicity. That had done the trick. They'd agreed to do a "well-being" check on Marilyn Bartlett.

An unmarked patrol car was parked in front of the house.

Pulling up in front of the home, Ava slid out of the vehicle happy to stretch her legs. She and Logan walked toward the door and were immediately greeted by a plainclothes police officer in the doorway. Clearly Wade wasn't here.

An older man with silver hair shook their hands. "I'm Detective Murray Townsend. You must be Logan Wright."

"I am, and this is my wife Ava. She also consults from time to time."

I do? How cool.

The captain didn't even question Ava's presence, getting straight to the point. "I must admit, Mr. Wright, I'm not sure why we're here. Has Dr. Bartlett broken any laws?"

"I don't know yet, but I am concerned for her safety. Wade Bryson is a dangerous man."

The man seemed dubious but accepted Logan's explanation. "Well, you're lucky my captain thinks so highly of the Anderson family. I can't think of anyone else that would be allowed to do this. We're breaking a couple of statutes right now."

Ava didn't care about the rules and Logan…well…he never had.

"I'm confident in my theory, Detective. I believe Marilyn Bartlett is in danger."

The older man shrugged. "If I get in trouble for this I'm throwing you under the bus. Anyway, I did a little checking while I was waiting for you. The female subject Dr. Bartlett isn't here, nor has she shown up for work. Her vehicle is not in the garage but the door to the garage was unlocked and from there I was able to enter the residence."

They'd need to put out a BOLO for the car.

"She didn't take her cell phone. I found that on her desk in the living room. There doesn't appear to have been any struggle, however. I see no evidence of any crime here."

"That doesn't mean she's with Wade Bryson voluntarily," Ava pointed out. "It just means she didn't fight back in this location."

"It could also mean that she's at the grocery store or visiting a friend and if she comes home and catches us inside of her house she'll sue the pants off of the department."

The detective was kind of a pessimist.

"Can we look around?" Logan asked. She could feel the leashed up tension in his body. He wanted...something to happen.

"Sure, why the hell not? We're already on thin ice. Just be quick. We have real crimes that need to be investigated. I'll wait outside. Don't take anything. I could get in big trouble for this."

The cop turned and exited the house.

"I don't think he believes your theory, husband."

"I don't give a shit what he believes. I should have just broken into the house. It would have been easier. Let's check out the kitchen."

Logan studied a wooden block of knives on the counter. One was missing.

"One of the knives is missing."

"But there's no blood anywhere that I can see." Logan opened the dishwasher. "And here it is. She really shouldn't put expensive knives in the dishwasher. She'll ruin them."

"You're kind of annoying at a possible crime scene."

Logan flashed her a grin. "I'm betting it's only going to become worse."

He opened the refrigerator and the contents were sparse. The pantry was stocked slightly more but it didn't look like Marilyn Bartlett liked to cook.

Opening a drawer, Logan pulled out a stack of well-worn

takeout menus. "Bingo. I bet she mostly ate out. So an empty refrigerator means nothing."

The rest of the kitchen didn't help so they moved into the living room. Ava headed straight for the desk where the cop said the cell phone had been found. She believed that desks and workspaces said a great deal about a person. For example, Ava's said that she was neat but impatient. Creative but orderly.

The doctor's desk was neat as well. A place for everything and everything in its place. Pens and pencils in the holder. Paper clips in a little open box. Even the rubber bands were stacked neatly.

If Marilyn Bartlett kept her work area this clean and organized that meant that all work had to put away in the drawers. She wouldn't leave it out. Sliding open the middle drawer, Ava found a planner open to the current week. Notations had been made on each day including exercise, water intake, and appointments. Dr. Bartlett has visited the dentist earlier this week. There was nothing there about Wade but they'd need to look through it completely.

"Logan, I found the doctor's daily planner."

"If she's anything like you she would have written down that she was planning to help a sociopath break out of prison. Monday, laundry. Tuesday, spinning class. Wednesday, help a serial killer. Thursday, book club."

So I might be a little detail oriented. Is that so wrong?

"Really? You're going to give me a hard time about my planner now? Is this really the time? You were right. You are more annoying."

"I think your planner is cute. Now what else can we find in this desk?"

"Was the doctor right or left handed?" Ava asked, standing in front of the desk. "There's a theory that everything important is always placed on the same side."

Thinking for a moment, Logan pointed to the right column of drawers. "She was right handed."

"Then let's try these first."

The top drawer was filled with receipts, probably for tax purposes, all clipped together in orderly little piles. The second drawer was almost empty, with nothing but a checkbook and an adding machine in it.

"I can't remember the last time I wrote a check," Ava said, picking it up and paging through the register. As expected, Dr. Bartlett was meticulous about recording every check written.

"Or used an adding machine. What's the date of the last entry?"

Ava held it up to show him. "About two years ago. She probably kept it for taxes."

"Check the bottom drawer."

Empty. The left column wasn't much better. After scouring the living room for a while longer, they made their way into the bedroom. Like the two rooms before, it was neat as a pin. The only item out of place was a recent hardback bestseller on the nightstand that Ava had recently finished reading. The book was facedown and open. A book lover, it drove Ava crazy when she saw people do this.

"She didn't have a freakin' book mark? She has a stack of post it notes on her desk. This poor book."

Ava lifted it, intending to see where in the story Dr. Bartlett had left off but there was something or *things*, plural, underneath it and they cascaded to the floor.

"Shit," Ava cursed, both her and Logan bending down to pick up what looked like a stack of photos. "I've got butterfingers."

Faster than she could ever hope to be, he had scooped up

most of the photos before she had a chance. "Baby, have I said that I love you today?"

He had.

"You did when I poured you coffee this morning. Why?"

He was grinning. That smile he was famous for, if only locally and among friends.

He held up one of the photos. "Look."

Ava had to look hard to see what he was smiling about, studying the photo carefully. When she did, her heart shifted into another gear and she had to remind herself to breathe. In and out. In and out.

Screw it, I'll breathe later. This is important now.

It was a picture of Lyle on that jogging path.

All of the pictures were of Lyle going about his day and they appeared to be taken from a distance, as if Dr. Bartlett had followed Lyle to study his daily schedule.

"I'll have Jared check to see if she has any firearms registered in her name. I'll have Jason call the authorities again as well. I think now I might have a little more credibility that Dr. Marilyn Bartlett, once a witness for the prosecution, shot and killed Lyle Bryson because his brother Wade wanted him dead. They might even believe that she helped him escape from prison and is on the run with him now."

Ava heard her husband speaking but the words barely penetrated her brain. She was too busy looking at the photos. There weren't many, maybe eight in total, but the more closely she looked at a few of them the more frightened she became until her heart was lodged in her throat. She grabbed Logan by the shirt, yanking it to get his attention.

She tapped on one of the pictures. "Look! It's not Lyle."

Logan took it from her hand and held it closer. "What do you mean? These are Lyle."

"No, *those* are Lyle." She pushed two other photos under his nose, her whole body shaking. The drive back to Corville would take too long. They'd have to call Drake. Thank heavens he'd stayed behind this morning due to some local business. "*These* are Aaron. Logan, she's not just after Lyle, she's after Aaron, too."

The brothers were close in age and looked very much alike.

It made sense. Wade hated the Bryson family dynasty and the business. He wouldn't choose one brother over the other. He'd want both of them gone.

The color drained from Logan's face and he quickly levered to his feet, dragging her with him. He was already running for the door with her on his heels. "Fuck, we need to get back there. Son of a fucking bitch."

Ava could only hope they'd figured it out in time.

CHAPTER THIRTY-THREE

The copper scent of blood hit Logan's nostrils when he walked up to the trunk of Aaron's car less than an hour later. He'd driven like a bat out of hell to get here but he'd known they were in no position to help as far away as they were. Drake and his deputies were Aaron's only hope and they hadn't made it in time.

No one would have. It was Aaron's habit a few days a week to come into the office very early, long before anyone else so he could work when it was quiet. It was then that he'd been shot in the head from close range. The shooter or shooters loaded the body in the trunk of Aaron's own car before driving away. It probably happened just as the sun was coming up.

The rest of the employees arrived one by one as Wade and Marilyn traveled farther away from the scene of the crime. If the employees noticed Aaron's car in the parking lot they didn't think much of it, even when he wasn't in his office. His assistant said that she thought his wife might have picked him up last night if he wasn't feeling well. A sick day would explain his absence this morning, although she admitted she was surprised he hadn't called. That's what had eventually led her to call

Lindsay and inquire about Aaron. When she'd found out that her boss was supposed to be in the office, she became extremely concerned and was about to call the police when Sheriff Drake and one of his deputies showed up. After a brief search, they'd found Aaron's body.

Logan edged in front of Ava, wanting to block her from seeing the grisly scene. He'd meant it that day so long ago at the wedding when he'd told her that seeing a dead body changed a person. She had seen dead bodies, but this was particularly awful. She didn't need these images keeping her awake at night.

"Are you doing this on purpose?" she asked, moving to her right. Logan simply stepped in front of her again.

"Yes. Why don't you wait inside the office?"

"I want to—"

"Trust me," he cut in. "You don't. Now go wait in the office. In fact, call Jared and see if he has anything for us."

Logan thought she was going to argue but to his surprise she agreed and went back into the building. Drake finished up with one of his deputies and the coroner made a few notes on a clipboard.

"According to the coroner he was shot in the head," Drake said, his own troubled expression mirroring Logan's. "He died instantly. He'll let us know what caliber gun as soon as possible."

The fact that Aaron had been shot in the head was incredibly obvious.

"I bet it will match the gun that shot Lyle," Logan replied. "If Marilyn Bartlett owns a gun, I bet it matches that, too."

Christ, this was such a fucking mess. Wade was evil, killing his own brothers. Logan would bet money that he'd done the deed this time. He'd want the adrenaline rush.

He'd want it again, though. And soon. Who would be next? Anyone in Wade's path was in danger.

✧　✧　✧　✧

Ava was cleaning up the kitchen after breakfast the next morning when she heard the sound of engines right outside the windows. Folding the dishtowel, she glanced outside and then did a double take. Several vehicles had just pulled into the driveway and at the front of the house. The men climbing out of those cars looked extremely familiar.

Seth. Tanner. Griffin. Reed. Dare. And…was that Jason and Jared, leading a German Shepherd?

Logan was in the backyard playing kickball with Brianna and Colt. The doors were wide open because of the good weather so she only had to call to get him inside. She welcomed the men before they even had a chance to knock, waving them inside.

"Looks like I better put on another pot of coffee," she said, giving each man a hug, one after the other. The dog, on the other hand, was the recipient of a suspicious look. Had Logan gone ahead and adopted a dog without discussing it with her? And now his friends were going to plead the canine's case? "To what do we owe the honor?"

"I'll second that question." Logan had come up behind her, but unlike her he'd given the dog a pet, getting a tail wag in return. "Jason. Jared. Did you come to tell me I'm no longer a partner in the firm?"

Not one man cracked a smile. They looked like they were heading to a funeral.

That's when it hit Ava.

God, I'm so stupid. They think it might be our funeral.

Ava drew a shaky breath, tears pricking the backs of her eyes. "I think I know why you're here."

Logan didn't look happy at all. His brows were pulled down into a straight line and a pulse jumped in his cheek. "Then tell me because I don't have a fucking clue."

He did. He was a smart man so he knew, but he was far into denial. They'd received word last night that Marilyn Bartlett did have a twenty-two registered in her name. It was also a twenty-two that killed both Aaron and Lyle. Those bullets matched. Dr. Bartlett was now wanted not only for aiding and abetting a fugitive but also double murder. Logan had solved Lyle's murder, after all. Not that Corville would be rejoicing in his victory.

"They're here because of Wade."

Tanner, the unofficial leader of the group, stepped forward. "Yes, because of Wade. He's a dangerous man, but not an unpredictable one. He's murdered his father, his uncle, and two of his brothers. Now there's only one left."

Logan.

Her husband wasn't going to give in gracefully. "I'm not part of the Bryson dynasty or any of their business dealings."

Reed stepped forward then. "True, and that's probably why you're still alive so far. But from what you've told us Wade wants to be you, wishes he was like you, and at the same time hates you. Eventually he's going to have to eliminate you because as long as you live he can't be the hero or god that he wants to be. We think you're next and we're here to take you and your family into protective custody until Wade, and any of his loony disciples, are caught."

Logan pointed to himself. "I'm going to get Wade but I wouldn't mind the help."

"No, buddy." Tanner shook his head sadly. "You and your family are going underground. Today. Right now. Only the seven of us plus Evan in Florida will know where you are. You'll stay under protection until Wade is back behind bars. Jason and Jared are going to escort you to a safe location along with Reed who will fly back here to help us."

Ava watched fascinated as a million expressions flitted across her beloved husband's face. The final one was determination.

"They can protect Ava and the kids but I'm not sitting on my ass while—"

"You won't be," Tanner interrupted. "You'll be helping with research and strategy. Tactics, however, will be carried out by my team. You want to see those kids graduate from high school? Get married? You want to sit in a rocking chair next to Ava and watch her hair turn gray then you'll listen to me. If that's not what you want, then feel free to tell me to go fuck myself. Your number one job while Wade is free is to protect your family, Logan. *Your family.* Let our number one job be catching him. You know you won't be able to let them out of your sight anyway, so why pretend otherwise?"

There was a long stretch of silence. Ava already knew the decision that needed to be made. She didn't have to like it but hopefully it wouldn't be for long. The sooner Wade was caught, the better.

"It's not your job," Logan said finally. "You don't even have anything to do with this. The Marshal service goes after fugitives."

"As of this morning, we've all been deputized," Seth said. "One of Evan's former colleagues is heading up the search and they could use all the help they can get. We're acting as the B team. That includes you, too. They're well aware that no one knows Wade Bryson's criminal habits better than you do."

A lump had built up in Ava's throat as she stared at this group of men she'd trust with her life. Strong, determined, honest, and stubborn as hell. They wouldn't give up until Wade had been found. They wouldn't let anything happen to her family. Her husband knew it, too.

"I'll give you one week," Logan growled. "And if you don't

have him then I'll go get him my damn self. One fucking week. That's it."

Tanner nodded. "One week. Hopefully it won't take any longer."

"Dare and I can help the kids pack," Griffin offered. "We need to get on the road."

Logan groaned and rolled his eyes. "Christ, we're not going in that motorhome again, are we? How old is that thing?"

Tanner finally smiled. "That motor home has been sold. We rented one in the name of Evan's publishing company. Damn thing is nicer than my first house, so don't bitch and moan. Now go pack. Griffin's right. We do need to get you on the road. The sooner you're out of any area that Wade might look for you, the better."

Ava felt safe with this group. No bad guys were going to get away from these determined men. When they worked together something...special happened. If anybody could keep them safe while at the same time finding a fugitive, it was these guys.

She'd tell the kids they were going on an adventure.

But wait...what about the dog?

"Um...I get why you are all here. But what's he here for?"

Seth let the dog move closer to Ava. She wasn't afraid of dogs or anything but she was rightfully wary as to whether they were friendly.

"It's a her, actually," Seth said with a grin, ruffling the dog's fur. "Her name is Molly. She trained to be a police dog but didn't quite make it. She's very well trained though, and will make an excellent line of protection for your family. Go ahead. Pet her. You're going to be her new mommy."

Ava shot Logan a dirty look. "Well, at least I don't have to give birth to this one. Are you sure you didn't cook this up with your friends just to get a dog?"

Raising out a tentative hand, she stroked Molly's silky fur and was rewarded by the canine eagerly snuggling against her hip and looking up at her with deep worshipful brown eyes.

It can't be all bad if someone looks at me like that. Being adored is nice.

"Are you ready?" Reed asked, his gaze darting between Ava and Logan. "We really do need to hurry. We have a long drive ahead of us."

That was the giant question. Was she ready? Being married to Logan Wright was never boring that was for sure.

"I'm ready. Let's do this."

I hope you enjoyed revisiting Logan and Ava! There's much more to come in the autumn of 2018. Thank you for reading Justice Divided!

Don't miss a thing! Sign up to be notified of Olivia's new releases:

oliviajaymesoptin.instapage.com

About the Author

Olivia Jaymes is a wife, mother, lover of sexy romance, and caffeine addict. She lives with her husband and son in central Florida and spends her days with handsome alpha males and spunky heroines.

She is currently working on a new contemporary romance series – The Hollywood Showmance Chronicles in addition to the ongoing Danger Incorporated series and the Cowboy Justice Association series.

Visit Olivia Jaymes at
www.OliviaJaymes.com

Other Titles by Olivia Jaymes

Danger Incorporated

Damsel In Danger
Hiding From Danger
Discarded Heart Novella
Indecent Danger
Embracing Danger
Danger In The Night
Reunited With Danger

Cowboy Justice Association

Cowboy Command
Justice Healed
Cowboy Truth
Cowboy Famous
Cowboy Cool
Imperfect Justice
The Deputies
Justice Inked
Justice Reborn
Vengeful Justice

Military Moguls

Champagne and Bullets
Diamonds and Revolvers
Caviar and Covert Ops
Emeralds, Rubies, and Camouflage

Midnight Blue Beach

Wicked After Midnight
Midnight Of No Return
Kiss Midnight Goodbye

The Hollywood Showmance Chronicles

A Kiss For the Cameras
Swinging From A Star
Wild on the Red Carpet
Love in the Spotlight